Echoes of Ravenscroft

David L. Waters

Published by David Waters, 2024.

This is a work of fiction. Similarities to real people, places, or events are entirely coincidental.

ECHOES OF RAVENSCROFT

First edition. November 25, 2024.

Copyright © 2024 David L. Waters.

ISBN: 979-8230979494

Written by David L. Waters.

Table of Contents

Echoes of Ravenscroft 1
Chapter 1: Introduction 2
Chapter 2: Inciting Incident 9
Chapter 3: Call to Action 18
Chapter 4: Meeting the Mentor 26
Chapter 5: Exploration 34
Chapter 6: First Challenge 44
Chapter 7: Gathering Allies 54
Chapter 8: Backstory 63
Chapter 9: Rising Tension 72
Chapter 10: Midpoint Reveal 82
Chapter 11: Crisis Point 90
Chapter 12: Dark Night of the Soul 98
Chapter 13: Plot Twist 106
Chapter 14: Resurrection 116
Chapter 15: Confrontation 126
Chapter 16: Climax 137
Chapter 17: Resolution 147
Chapter 18: Returning Home 156
Chapter 19: Reflection 166
Chapter 20: Epilogue 176

Dedication

To the seekers of truth and the brave souls who dare to look beyond the veil,

This book is dedicated to those who embrace the mysteries of the unknown and the echoes of the past. May you find courage in the face of the supernatural, and may your quest for understanding guide you through the shadows to the light. Your journey is as timeless as the tales whispered through the halls of Ravenscroft.

Epigraph

"In the shadows of the past lie the echoes of forgotten truths, waiting to be unveiled by those who dare to listen." — Unknown

Echoes of Ravenscroft: Blackwood Explores an Enigmatic Location

Chapter 1: Introduction

The gas lamps flickered weakly as Detective Arthur Blackwood approached the imposing townhouse, its windows dark save for a faint glow emanating from the study. His footsteps echoed hollowly on the cobblestones, each sound muffled by the thick fog that clung to the streets of London like a funeral shroud.

Blackwood paused at the threshold, steeling himself. "Steel your nerves, old boy," he muttered. "What horrors await beyond?"

With a steadying breath, he pushed open the heavy oak door. It creaked ominously, as if warning him to turn back. But Blackwood pressed on, driven by an inexorable need to uncover the truth.

The study lay at the end of a long corridor. As Blackwood entered, the silence enveloped him, broken only by the soft ticking of a grandfather clock. His eyes, accustomed to peering through London's misty veil, struggled to pierce the gloom.

Then he saw it.

A choked gasp escaped his lips as the full horror of the scene unveiled itself. The walls, once adorned with scholarly tomes, now bore a macabre new decoration - great swathes of crimson, still glistening wetly in the dim light.

"Good God," Blackwood whispered, his blood running cold. "What manner of fiend could have perpetrated such an atrocity?"

His gaze traveled the room, taking in every gruesome detail. The blood formed intricate patterns, almost beautiful in their terrible symmetry. It was as if some deranged artist had used Professor Winthrop's lifeblood as his medium, creating a nightmarish masterpiece.

Blackwood's mind reeled, grappling with the implications. What dark purpose lay behind this savagery? What message was the killer trying to convey?

He took a tentative step forward, his keen eyes searching for any clue that might shed light on this infernal mystery. But even as his analytical mind began to work, Blackwood felt a primal fear stirring in his breast.

Something unnatural had occurred here.

Something that defied rational explanation.

And as the shadows seemed to deepen around him, Blackwood knew with chilling certainty that he had stumbled upon a case that would test his deductive skills and the foundations of his sanity.

As Blackwood approached the study desk, a new sensation assaulted his senses. A faint, cloying scent hung in the air, barely perceptible beneath the metallic tang of blood.

"Incense," he murmured, his brow furrowing. "How peculiar."

He leaned closer, inhaling deeply. The fragrance was exotic, unfamiliar. It spoke of distant lands and arcane rituals. Blackwood's mind raced, connecting this new piece of evidence to the gruesome tableau surrounding him.

"Could this have been some sort of... ceremony?" he wondered aloud, his voice barely above a whisper.

His piercing blue eyes swept the room again, taking in details he had initially overlooked in his shock. The professor's chair lay overturned, papers strewn across the floor. A bookshelf had been emptied partially, its contents scattered haphazardly.

"Signs of a struggle," Blackwood muttered, his keen mind reconstructing the scene. "But was it resistance or part of the ritual itself?"

He maneuvered around the desk, mindful not to disturb any potential evidence. His gaze fell upon a leather-bound tome, its pages open to an illustration of arcane symbols.

"What secrets were you pursuing, Professor?" Blackwood asked the empty room. "And did they lead to your demise?"

As he continued his examination, a chill ran down his spine. The feeling of being watched, which had plagued him since entering the house, intensified. Blackwood straightened, his hand instinctively moving to the revolver concealed beneath his coat.

"I am not alone here," he thought, his heart quickening. "But is my unseen companion of this world or another?"

A glint of metal caught Blackwood's eye, drawing his attention to the floor near the overturned chair. He crouched down, his keen gaze fixed upon the object.

"Good Lord," he breathed, carefully lifting a bloodstained knife from the carpet. The ornate handle was unlike anything he had encountered before; its design was intricate and foreign.

Blackwood turned the blade over in his gloved hands, studying it intently. "Not a common weapon," he mused aloud. "Custom-made, perhaps? But for what purpose?"

The Detective's mind raced with possibilities. Could this be the murder weapon? Or was it merely a prop in some arcane ritual? The blood coating the blade seemed to suggest the former, but in Blackwood's experience, appearances could be deceiving.

He placed the knife carefully on the desk, making a mental note to have it examined thoroughly. As he did so, his instincts prickled. Something about this room felt... off. His years of experience had taught him to trust these hunches.

"If I were hiding something in a study," Blackwood muttered, running his hand along the wood paneling, "where would I conceal it?"

His fingers probed every crevice, every join in the woodwork. He tapped gently on the walls, listening for any hollow sounds that might betray a hidden compartment.

"Come now, Professor," he said softly, addressing the deceased academic. "You were a man of secrets. Surely you wouldn't leave them all in plain sight?"

As if in answer to his query, Blackwood's hand brushed against a slight protrusion in one of the panels. A wall section swung inward with a soft click, revealing a narrow passage beyond.

Blackwood's heart raced with excitement and trepidation. "Well, well," he whispered, peering into the darkness. "What other mysteries do you have in store for me, I wonder?"

As Blackwood took a tentative step towards the hidden passage, a sudden chill coursed through his body, causing him to shudder involuntarily. The hairs on the back of his neck stood on end and an overwhelming sense of being watched washed over him.

"Who's there?" he called out, his voice steady despite the unease gripping his heart. The shadows in the room's corners deepened as if in response to his query.

Blackwood's hand instinctively moved to the revolver holstered at his hip. "I've faced my share of spectral entities," he thought, his mind racing. "But this... this feels different."

He turned slowly, surveying the room with heightened alertness. His gaze swept across the bookshelves and the blood-spattered desk and finally came to rest on a large portrait hanging on the far wall. The painting depicted a woman of striking beauty, her regal bearing unmistakable even in oils.

"Lady Eleanor Ravenscroft," Blackwood breathed, recognition dawning. "But how...?"

He approached the portrait, drawn by an inexplicable compulsion. The woman's eyes seemed to follow him, filled with sorrow and urgency that transcended the canvas.

"I've seen your face before," Blackwood murmured, addressing the painting. "In the archives of unsolved cases. You vanished without a trace over a century ago."

A flicker of movement caught his eye, and Blackwood could have sworn he saw the painted lips move ever so slightly.

"Am I losing my mind?" he wondered aloud, rubbing his temples. "Or is there more to this mystery than meets the eye?"

The room grew colder still, and Blackwood couldn't shake the feeling that Lady Ravenscroft was trying to communicate with him from beyond the grave.

As Blackwood turned away from the portrait, a shimmering mist merged in the center of the room. His breath caught in his throat as the ethereal form of Lady Eleanor Ravenscroft materialized before him, her spectral beauty both captivating and chilling.

"Detective Blackwood," her voice echoed, tinged with an otherworldly resonance. "I implore you; do not dismiss what your eyes perceive."

Blackwood's hand trembled slightly as he adjusted his stance. "Lady Ravenscroft," he said, his voice steady despite his racing heart. "I've encountered spirits before, but never one so... corporeal. What brings you to this grim scene?"

The ghost's face contorted with anguish, her translucent form shimmering in the dim light.

"The professor's death is but a thread in a tapestry of darkness," she whispered. "The Order of the Eternal Flame has awakened, Detective. Their nefarious intentions threaten not just this world but the very fabric of existence."

Blackwood's mind reeled. The Order of the Eternal Flame—a name whispered in the darkest corners of occult lore. "How is this possible?" he thought. "And why reveal this to me?"

Aloud, he asked, "My lady, what connection does this Order have to Professor Winthrop's murder? And how can I, a mere mortal, hope to stand against such hostility?"

Lady Ravenscroft's ethereal form drifted closer, her eyes locking with Blackwood's. "You possess a rare gift, Detective—the ability to bridge the gap between worlds. The Order seeks an artifact hidden within these walls that could unleash untold horrors upon London and beyond."

Blackwood felt a chill run down his spine, not from the ghostly presence before him but from the task's weight at his feet. "I'm no hero, my lady," he said softly. "But I cannot ignore such a plea. Tell me, what must I do to unravel this mystery and thwart the Order's plans?"

Lady Ravenscroft's spectral form wavered, her voice tinged with relief. "Your willingness to aid our cause brings hope, Detective Blackwood.

Seek the truth hidden within these bloodstained walls."

Blackwood nodded solemnly, his piercing blue eyes scanning the room with renewed purpose.

"I shall do my utmost, my lady. The Order will not triumph while I draw breath."

As Lady Ravenscroft faded from view, Blackwood turned his attention to the grisly scene before him. The coppery scent of blood mingled with the lingering aroma of incense, creating a nauseating perfume of death and ritual.

"What secrets did you uncover, Professor Winthrop?" Blackwood muttered, carefully stepping around the congealing pools of crimson. His keen gaze swept over the study, noting the smallest details—a misplaced book, a scratched floorboard, a torn piece of parchment peeking out from beneath the heavy oak desk.

As he bent to retrieve the fragment, Blackwood's mind raced. "The Order must have been searching for something specific. But what could be so valuable as to warrant such brutality?"

His fingers closed around the parchment, and a jolt of energy coursed through him. Blackwood stumbled back, his vision blurring momentarily.

When it cleared, he stared at a series of cryptic symbols etched onto the aged paper.

"By Jove," he whispered, tracing the intricate designs with a trembling finger. "What manner of arcane knowledge have I stumbled upon?"

A sudden wind extinguished the nearby candles, plunging the study into darkness.

Blackwood's heart raced his senses on high alert. He could have sworn he heard a faint whisper in the shadows—a chilling promise of retribution from unseen watchers.

"I must tread carefully," Blackwood thought, pocketing the parchment. "The Order's reach may extend further than I imagined. Every step forward could lead me closer to the truth or my demise."

Chapter 2: Inciting Incident

The flickering gas lamp cast long shadows across the study as Detective Arthur Blackwood entered, his footsteps muffled by the thick Oriental rug. The metallic scent of blood assaulted his senses, causing his stomach to churn. He paused, allowing his eyes to adjust to the dim light.

"Good God," he muttered, taking in the grisly tableau.

Professor Winthrop's body lay sprawled across his mahogany desk, limbs akimbo, papers scattered about like fallen leaves. The once-immaculate waistcoat was now stained with a deep crimson. Blackwood approached slowly, his keen gaze sweeping the room.

How swiftly the veil of civility can be torn away, he mused. Even in this sanctuary of learning, violence finds its way.

"What secrets did you uncover, old friend?"

Blackwood murmured, leaning in to examine the professor's lifeless form. "What darkness pursued you?"

The Detective's eyes narrowed as he noted the savagery of the attack. Multiple stab wounds peppered the victim's torso, speaking of a frenzied assault rather than a calculated hit.

Blackwood straightened, turning his attention to the blood-spattered walls. Crimson arcs and spatters formed a macabre canvas, each droplet a potential clue. He moved methodically, scrutinizing every inch.

"The killer was right-handed," he observed aloud, tracing the angle of a particularly vivid spray. "And of considerable strength, judging by the force required."

As he continued his examination, Blackwood's mind raced. What could drive someone to such brutality against a respected academic? What forbidden knowledge had Winthrop stumbled upon?

The distant tolling of church bells drifted through the window, a somber reminder of the world beyond this chamber of horrors.

Blackwood sighed heavily, the weight of the investigation settling upon his shoulders.

"I'll find the truth, Algernon," he vowed softly. "Whatever the cost."

A sudden, inexplicable chill crept up his spine as Blackwood's gaze swept the room again. He froze, every muscle tensing as the familiar sensation washed over him. The air grew heavy, charged with an otherworldly presence that set his teeth on edge.

"Not here," he whispered, his breath misting in the suddenly frigid air. "Not now."

Years of experience had honed Blackwood's intuition, teaching him to trust these preternatural instincts. He closed his eyes, allowing his other senses to guide him. The scent of blood faded, replaced by a faint, ethereal fragrance he couldn't quite place.

"Show yourself," Blackwood murmured, his voice steady despite the rapid pounding of his heart. "I know you're here."

The temperature plummeted further, frost forming on the window panes. A faint, shimmering light began to merge in the corner of his eye. Blackwood turned slowly, his hand instinctively moving to the revolver at his hip.

"By God," he breathed, eyes widening as the light took form. Fear and fascination warred within him, each heartbeat thundering in his ears. "What manner of spirit are you?"

The apparition before him pulsed with an otherworldly radiance, its edges blurred and shifting. Blackwood steeled himself, years of facing the unknown lending him strength.

"Speak if you can," he commanded, his voice carrying more confidence than he felt. "Why have you come?"

As the ghostly form solidified, Blackwood's mind raced. What connection did this spectral visitor have to the grisly scene around them? And what dark truths would its presence unveil?

The shimmering light coalesced into the figure of a woman, her translucent form exuding an ethereal beauty that left Blackwood momentarily breathless. Lady Eleanor Ravenscroft stood before him, her spectral presence both captivating and haunting. Her eyes, pools of infinite sorrow, locked onto Blackwood's, silently pleading for his attention.

Blackwood felt a jolt of recognition. "Lady Ravenscroft," he whispered, his voice barely audible in the oppressive silence of the study.

Despite the shock coursing through his veins, he maintained his composure, years of confronting the supernatural steeling his nerves.

With a respectful nod, he addressed the ghostly figure. "My lady, to what do I owe this... unexpected visitation?"

Lady Ravenscroft's lips parted, her voice carrying an echo of centuries past. "Detective Blackwood, I come to you in a time of great need."

Blackwood listened intently, his mind racing to process the surreal situation. He'd encountered spirits before, but never one so clearly defined, so purposeful in its manifestation.

"I'm listening, my lady," he said, his tone measured and calm despite the turmoil within.

"How may I serve one from beyond the veil?"

As Lady Ravenscroft began to speak, Blackwood was captivated by the melancholy grace of her spectral form. He couldn't help but wonder what tragic tale had led to her restless wandering between worlds.

"The truth, Detective," she intoned, her voice laden with urgency. "It lies buried beneath layers of deceit and darkness. You must uncover it for both the living and the dead."

Blackwood's brow furrowed. "The truth about this murder, you mean?" he asked, gesturing to the gruesome scene around them. "Or is there more at stake here?"

Lady Ravenscroft's ethereal form shimmered, her eyes burning with an otherworldly intensity.

"Professor Winthrop's death is a single thread in a tapestry of malevolence, Detective. His murder is inextricably linked to the ancient Order of the Eternal Flame."

Blackwood's pulse quickened, his mind racing to process this revelation. "The Order of the Eternal Flame?" he repeated, his voice barely above a whisper. "I've heard whispers, nothing more. What connection could the professor have had with such an enigmatic group?"

The apparition's voice grew more urgent, the air around them seeming to pulse with each syllable. "Time is of the essence, Detective. The Order's influence reaches far beyond the mortal realm. They seek power that should remain dormant, locked away from human hands."

As Lady Ravenscroft spoke, Blackwood's keen mind began piecing together fragments of information, like shards of a shattered mirror slowly reforming. The professor's obsession with obscure historical texts, his recent secretive behavior, and the strange symbols etched into the margins of his notes began to merge into a chilling picture.

"Good God," Blackwood muttered, running a hand through his tousled hair. "This case... it's far more complex than I initially thought. We're dealing with forces beyond the natural world, right?"

Lady Ravenscroft nodded solemnly, her form flickering like a candle in a draft. "You begin to understand, Detective. The veil between worlds grows thin, and dark forces gather strength. You must act swiftly, lest the balance be irrevocably upset."

Blackwood's eyes narrowed, his resolve hardening. "I've faced the supernatural before, my lady, but never on this scale. What am I to do? Where do I even begin to unravel such a mystery?"

The ghost's voice softened, a hint of compassion tempering her urgency. "Trust your instincts, Detective Blackwood. They have served you well in the past. Seek out the hidden truths in the professor's research. The answers you need, lie within the shadows of history."

As the task's weight settled upon him, Blackwood couldn't help but feel a mix of trepidation and exhilaration. This case would test him like no other, pushing him to the limits of his abilities and beliefs.

Blackwood's piercing blue eyes locked onto Lady Ravenscroft's ethereal form. "You speak of the Order of the Eternal Flame," he said, his voice low and measured. "What connection did Professor Winthrop have to this ancient society?"

The apparition's form wavered, her sorrow-filled eyes seeming to look beyond Blackwood to some distant, unseen point. "The professor... he sought knowledge not meant for mortal minds," she whispered, her voice carrying an otherworldly echo. "He delved too deep into the Order's secrets, uncovering truths that have lain dormant for centuries."

Blackwood's brow furrowed, his mind racing to piece together the fragments of information.

"And these secrets," he pressed, "they posed a threat to someone, didn't they? Someone powerful enough to silence him permanently."

Lady Ravenscroft's spectral form seemed to pulse with an inner light as she spoke. "The Order's influence reaches far beyond the veil of this world, Detective. They guard their mysteries with unholy fervor."

As he listened, Blackwood felt a familiar stirring within him—a mixture of dread and fascination that had accompanied his previous encounters with the supernatural. He knew, with a certainty that chilled him to his core, that he could not turn away from this case.

"I've faced dark forces before," he murmured, more to himself than to the ghost. "But this... this feels different. Larger. More perilous."

Lady Ravenscroft's voice softened, a hint of compassion tempering her urgency. "You stand at a crossroads, Detective Blackwood. The path ahead is fraught with danger, but you possess the intuition to navigate it."

Blackwood squared his shoulders, his resolve hardening. "Then I have no choice but to accept your plea, my lady. I will uncover the truth, no matter the cost."

As the words left Blackwood's lips, Lady Ravenscroft's form began to shimmer, her edges blurring into the dim light of the study.

Her eyes, filled with gratitude and sorrow, locked onto his.

"Remember, Detective," she whispered, her voice fading like a distant echo, "the veil between worlds is thinner than most believe.

Trust your instincts; they will guide you where mortal eyes cannot see."

Blackwood stood transfixed, watching as the last wisps of her ethereal presence dissipated into the air. The room seemed to exhale, the oppressive weight of the supernatural lifting, leaving behind only the lingering scent of decay and the metallic tang of blood.

"I give you my word, Lady Ravenscroft," he murmured into the space. "I shall not rest until justice is served for both the living and the dead."

The Detective remained motionless momentarily, his keen eyes scanning the room as if committing every detail to memory. The gravity of the task before him settled upon his shoulders like a leaden cloak.

"By God," Blackwood muttered, running a hand through his tousled hair, "what have I entangled myself in this time?"

He paced the length of the study, and the plush carpet muffled his footsteps. The case before him was unlike any he had encountered, a labyrinth of occult mysteries and mortal dangers. Blackwood knew that to navigate it, he would need to draw upon every skill he had honed over his years of detective work and perhaps even abilities he had yet to discover within himself.

"The Order of the Eternal Flame," he mused aloud, barely above a whisper. "What secrets do you guard so jealously? And at what cost?"

With a sharp inhale, Blackwood steeled himself and began his methodical search of the study. His piercing blue eyes swept across the room, taking in the chaos of scattered papers and overturned furniture with practiced precision.

"Every object tells a story," he murmured, crouching to examine a fallen book. "What tale do you wish to impart, I wonder?"

He lifted the tome, noting its ancient leather binding and the curious symbol embossed on its cover—a flame encircled by an Ouroboros.

"The Order's insignia, perhaps?" Blackwood mused, carefully placing the book on the desk.

As he sifted through the debris, his thoughts raced. "Lady Ravenscroft spoke of a connection between the professor and this Order. But what could link a respected academic to an ancient occult society?"

His keen gaze fell upon a half-burnt letter in the fireplace. He gingerly retrieved the fragile parchment with gloved hands, his brow furrowing as he deciphered the few legible words.

"'Beware the Crimson Moon,'" Blackwood read aloud, his voice tinged with curiosity. "A warning? Or a threat?"

He pocketed the charred remnant, his mind already formulating theories. The Detective's practiced hands continued their search, carefully examining each potential clue.

"There must be more," he muttered, frustration creeping into his tone. "What am I missing?"

As the first hints of dawn began to seep through the heavy curtains, Blackwood straightened, casting one final, penetrating glance around the room. The weight of unresolved questions hung heavy in the air.

"Time to take this investigation to the streets," he declared, adjusting his coat. With a deep breath, he stepped out of the study and into the fog-laden corridors of London, ready to plunge deeper into the enigma that had trapped him.

Detective Arthur Blackwood stepped out into the fogbound streets of London, the chill air nipping at his face. The gas lamps flickered feebly, their light barely penetrating the thick mist that cloaked the city. As he walked, his footsteps echoed hollowly on the cobblestones, muffled by the oppressive fog.

"Curious," he murmured, piercing blue eyes scanning the deserted street. "Even the most hardened criminals seem to have retreated from this unnatural gloom."

His mind raced with the implications of Lady Ravenscroft's spectral visitation. The Order of the Eternal Flame, Professor Winthrop's brutal murder, and the cryptic warning about the Crimson Moon - all pieces of a puzzle he was determined to solve.

As he turned a corner, the silhouette of a hunched figure emerged from the mist.

Blackwood's hand instinctively moved to his coat pocket, where he kept his revolver.

"Who goes there?" he called out, his voice steady despite the tension in his chest.

The figure shuffled closer, revealing itself to be an elderly street sweeper. "Begging your pardon, sir," the old man wheezed. "Didn't mean to startle ye. Nasty night for a walk, isn't it?"

Blackwood relaxed slightly but remained alert.

"Indeed, it is. Tell me, have you noticed anything... unusual tonight?"

The street sweeper's rheumy eyes widened.

"Unusual, ye say? Well, now that ye mention it, I did see somethin' queer-like. A group of gentlemen, all dressed in black, hurryin' down towards the river. Looked like they were carryin' somethin' heavy, they did."

Blackwood's interest piqued. "Towards the river, you say? How long ago was this?"

"Not more'n an hour past, I reckon," the old man replied, leaning on his broom.

"Thank you, my good man. You've been most helpful," Blackwood said, pressing a coin into the sweeper's gnarled hand.

As he strode purposefully towards the Thames, Blackwood's thoughts churned. "Could these men be connected to the Order? And what were they transporting so secretively?"

The fog thickened as he neared the river, the damp air clinging to his clothes. The distant sound of lapping water grew louder, and a faint, eerie glow began to penetrate the mist.

Blackwood's heart raced as he approached the source of the light. "By all that's holy," he whispered, his eyes widening at the sight before him.

Chapter 3: Call to Action

Detective Arthur Blackwood stood motionless in Professor Winthrop's study, his eyes struggling to pierce the gloom. A single gas lamp cast flickering shadows across the room, illuminating the gruesome tableau before him. The professor's body lay crumpled behind his ornate mahogany desk, a dark stain spreading across the Persian rug beneath him.

Blackwood's piercing blue eyes darted from the corpse to the scattered papers and overturned chair. His mind raced, each observation birthing a new, unsettling question: What force could have overcome the esteemed scholar, and to what end?

He moved cautiously through the room, and the thick carpet muffled his footsteps. "What secrets did you uncover, old friend?" he murmured, his voice barely above a whisper.

A chill wind swept through the study as if in answer, extinguishing the lamp's faltering flame.

Blackwood's hand instinctively moved to the revolver at his hip, his body tensing as he peered into the darkness.

A soft, ethereal glow began to merge in the corner of the room, gradually taking on a human form. Blackwood's breath caught in his throat as the apparition of a woman materialized before him. Her translucent figure radiated an otherworldly beauty, her features noble and tinged with sorrow.

"Detective Blackwood," she spoke, her voice a whisper that seemed to echo through time. "I am Lady Eleanor Ravenscroft. I implore you to uncover the truth behind Professor Winthrop's demise."

Blackwood's mind reeled, torn between his rational training and the undeniable evidence of his senses. He had encountered the supernatural before, but never so directly or compellingly.

"My lady," he managed, his usual measured tones betraying a hint of awe, "how do you know of this tragedy? And why come to me?"

Lady Ravenscroft's form shimmered, her eyes meeting Blackwood's with an intensity that seemed to pierce his soul. "The threads of fate are tangled, Detective. The professor's death is one knot in a tapestry of darkness stretching centuries. You alone possess the insight to unravel this mystery."

Blackwood's brow furrowed, his analytical mind already beginning to piece together fragments of information. "The professor's research," he mused aloud, "dealt with ancient orders and forgotten lore. Did he stumble upon something he was not meant to know?"

"You perceive truly," Lady Ravenscroft nodded, her spectral form drifting closer. "But time grows short, and forces beyond your understanding are already moving to conceal the truth. Will you take up this task, Detective Blackwood? Will you seek justice for the professor and countless souls trapped in the shadows of history?"

Blackwood squared his shoulders, his resolve crystallizing. "I shall, my lady. Whatever the cost, whatever dangers lie ahead, I will uncover the truth behind this foul deed."

As Lady Ravenscroft's form began to fade, her voice lingered in the air. "Then go forth, Detective. The fog-shrouded streets of London hold many secrets. Some truths are written in blood, others whispered by the dead. Trust your instincts, for they will guide you through the darkness ahead."

She vanished with a final, haunting smile, leaving Blackwood alone in the shadowy study. He turned back to the grim scene before him, his mind already formulating a plan of action.

Whatever forces were at play, whatever ancient evils stirred in the night, Arthur Blackwood would not rest until justice was served and the truth brought to light.

Blackwood's piercing blue eyes narrowed, his gaze fixed on the spot where Lady Ravenscroft's ethereal form had vanished. A chill ran down his spine, not entirely because of the ghostly encounter. He ran a hand through his tousled dark hair, his mind grappling with the reality of what he'd just witnessed.

"A spirit," he murmured, his voice barely above a whisper. "Seeking justice from beyond the grave. It defies all logic, and yet..."

He turned back to the gruesome scene, the professor's lifeless body a stark reminder of the very tangible crime at hand. Blackwood's analytical mind warred with the undeniable pull of intuition that had served him well in past cases.

"What say you, Detective?" The gruff voice of Inspector Hawkins broke through Blackwood's reverie. "Found any of your... unusual clues?"

Blackwood's lips tightened. "Perhaps, Inspector. Though I doubt you'd put much stock in them."

Hawkins scoffed. "Spare me your ghost stories and give me something I can use in a proper investigation."

As the inspector lumbered away, Blackwood's thoughts raced. The urgency in Lady Ravenscroft's plea echoed in his mind, intertwined with the risks of pursuing such an unconventional lead. His reputation, already hanging by a thread because of his unorthodox methods, could be irreparably damaged.

"And yet," he mused inwardly, "if there's even a grain of truth to her words, the consequences of inaction could be dire."

Blackwood paced the room, and the thick carpet muffled his footsteps. "Logic dictates I focus on the physical evidence, the mundane aspects of the crime. But my instincts..." He paused, glancing at a shadowy corner where he could almost imagine Lady Ravenscroft's form lingering. "My instincts have never led me astray, no matter how improbable the path."

He approached the professor's desk, fingers tracing the edge of an ancient tome. "What secrets did you uncover, old friend? And what price did you pay for that knowledge?"

Blackwood's eyes closed, his mind drifting to past encounters that defied rational explanation. The banshee's wail that had saved a family from certain doom, the spectral hound that led him to a murderer's lair, the whispering portraits that revealed long-buried secrets. Each memory strengthened his resolve, cementing his determination to unravel the mystery.

"I cannot turn away," he murmured, his voice barely audible in the oppressive silence of the study. "For the professor's sake and for Lady Ravenscroft's, I must see this through."

With renewed purpose, Blackwood turned his attention to the scattered papers on the desk.

His eyes scanned the documents, searching for any mention of the Order of the Eternal Flame.

"The Order," he mused aloud, "what connection could it have to Winthrop's demise?"

A cold draft whispered through the room as if in response, causing the papers to flutter.

Blackwood's gaze sharpened, focusing on a partially obscured symbol—a flame encircled by an Ouroboros.

"Curious," he muttered, carefully extracting the page. "Winthrop, what were you delving into?"

He began to piece together fragments of information, his mind working methodically to construct a narrative. Dates, locations, and cryptic references slowly coalesced into a pattern.

"The Order's roots run deep," Blackwood said, addressing the empty room. "Centuries of influence, hidden just beneath the surface of our world. But why target Winthrop now?"

A soft, ethereal voice responded, startling him.

"Because he was close to uncovering their greatest secret."

Blackwood turned to face Lady Ravenscroft's shimmering form. "And what secret might that be, my lady?"

Her eyes, filled with otherworldly wisdom, met his. "The power to bridge the gap between the living and the dead, Detective. A power they would kill to protect."

Blackwood's eyes widened, the weight of Lady Ravenscroft's words sinking into his core. At that moment, the pieces of the puzzle snapped into place with startling clarity.

"Good God," he breathed, running a hand through his tousled hair. "The Order isn't just some arcane society—they're gatekeepers of life and death itself."

His mind raced, connections forming rapidly.

"Winthrop's research, his obsession with ancient rituals... he must have stumbled upon their secrets."

Lady Ravenscroft's form flickered, her voice urgent. "You understand now, Detective. The gravity of what we face."

Blackwood nodded solemnly. "Indeed, my lady. And it seems I've unwittingly stepped into a war between worlds."

With newfound purpose, he gathered vital documents from Winthrop's desk. His movements were deliberate, each paper carefully selected and tucked into his coat.

"If I'm to unravel this mystery," he muttered, "I'll need to trace the Order's history. Their origins may hold the key to their current machinations."

As he prepared to leave, Blackwood paused, his hand resting on an ornate letter opener.

"Lady Ravenscroft, I fear this investigation may lead me down treacherous paths. Are you certain you wish me to continue?"

The spectral figure's eyes gleamed with determination. "More than ever, Detective. The truth must be uncovered, no matter the cost."

Blackwood nodded, his resolve strengthened.

"Then let us begin. I believe I know where to start our search for answers."

With a final glance around the study, he strode towards the door, his mind already formulating a plan to delve deeper into the enigma that had trapped him.

As Blackwood stepped out of Professor Winthrop's study, he was immediately enveloped by a thick, cloying fog that seemed to cling to his skin. The gas lamps along the street flickered weakly, their light barely penetrating the oppressive gloom. Each shadow loomed large and menacing as if concealing untold dangers within its murky depths.

"Good God," Blackwood muttered, his breath forming ghostly wisps in the frigid air. "It's as if London itself conspires to shroud this mystery."

He stood for a moment, his keen eyes scanning the deserted street. The fog muffled all sound, creating an eerie silence broken only by the distant, hollow echo of his footsteps on the cobblestones.

"I must press on," he thought, his jaw set with determination. "Lady Ravenscroft's plight weighs heavily upon me, and I cannot falter now."

As he began to navigate the fog-laden streets, Blackwood's mind raced with the implications of what he had uncovered. The Order of the Eternal Flame, Winthrop's murder, and the spectral pleas of Lady Ravenscroft—all pieces of a puzzle that threatened to shake the foundations of his understanding of the world.

"What manner of force am I truly contending with?" he wondered, his brow furrowed in concentration. "And how deep do the Order's roots truly run in our fair city?"

A sudden gust of wind momentarily parted the fog, revealing a shadowy figure at the far end of the street. Blackwood's hand instinctively moved to the revolver concealed beneath his coat.

"Who goes there?" he called out, his voice steady despite the tension within him.

The figure made no reply, instead melting back into the mist as swiftly as it had appeared.

"Perhaps merely a trick of the light," Blackwood mused, unconvinced. "Or a warning of the dangers that lie ahead."

He pressed on, and each step was measured and purposeful. The weight of his responsibility to the living and the dead drove him forward, even as the fog seemed to press in from all sides, threatening to swallow him whole.

"I swear to you, Lady Ravenscroft," he whispered into the night, "I shall uncover the truth, no matter the cost to myself. Your restless spirit shall find peace, and justice will be served."

With renewed resolve, Detective Arthur Blackwood vanished into the murky labyrinth of Victorian London, the first threads of a centuries-old conspiracy beginning to unravel before him.

As Blackwood rounded a corner, the muffled sound of footsteps echoed off the damp cobblestones. A familiar silhouette emerged from the mist, revealing the weathered face of Inspector Graves.

"Blackwood? What in blazes are you doing out at this ungodly hour?" Graves demanded, his bushy eyebrows furrowing.

Blackwood's piercing blue eyes met the inspector's gaze. "Following a lead, Graves.

One that may shed light on the professor's murder."

Graves scoffed, "Don't tell me you're chasing ghosts again, man. The higher-ups are already questioning your methods."

"And what if I am?" Blackwood replied, his voice low and measured. "There are forces at work here beyond our mortal understanding."

"Listen to yourself!" Graves exclaimed. "This obsession with the supernatural will be your undoing, mark my words."

Blackwood's jaw tightened. "I've solved cases deemed impossible before, Graves. This one will be no different."

As Graves shook his head in dismay, Blackwood's thoughts raced. "If only he could see what I've witnessed," he mused internally.

"The veil between worlds is thinner than most realize."

"Just... be careful, Blackwood," Graves sighed. "And for heaven's sake, try to find evidence that doesn't involve spectral witnesses."

With a curt nod, Blackwood continued, leaving the skeptical inspector behind. His destination loomed ahead—a decrepit church, its spire barely visible through the fog.

"The Order of the Eternal Flame," Blackwood whispered as he approached the weathered doors. "What secrets lie hidden within your hallowed walls?"

His heart pounded with anticipation as he placed his hand on the ancient wood.

Whatever awaited him beyond this threshold, Blackwood knew it would irrevocably alter the course of his investigation—and perhaps his understanding of reality itself.

Chapter 4: Meeting the Mentor

As he approached Agnes O'Reilly's boarding house, the fog clung to Detective Arthur Blackwood like a spectral shroud. Each footfall on the damp cobblestones echoed ominously as if the very streets of London were whispering dark secrets. Blackwood paused at the threshold, his piercing blue eyes scanning the weathered facade. The weight of his investigation pressed upon him, urging caution.

"Steady on, old boy," he muttered, inhaling deeply. The chill air filled his lungs, carrying the acrid scent of coal smoke and something more elusive - a hint of danger, perhaps?

Steeling his nerves, Blackwood raised a gloved hand and rapped sharply on the door. The sound reverberated through the foggy silence, seeming suspended in the air. As he waited, his mind raced with possibilities. What new threads might Agnes provide to unravel this infernal mystery?

The door creaked open, dispelling the gloom with a warm glow from within. Agnes O'Reilly stood framed in the doorway, her silver hair neatly coiffed and her eyes twinkling with wisdom and concern.

"Detective Blackwood," she greeted him, her voice as soothing as a lullaby. "Do come in out of this dreadful fog, dear."

Blackwood felt the tension in his shoulders ease slightly as he stepped over the threshold. "Mrs. O'Reilly, I apologize for the late hour. I hope I'm not intruding."

"Nonsense," Agnes chided gently, ushering him inside. "You're always welcome here. I can see the weight of your troubles, love. Let's get you settled, and we'll see what can be done."

Blackwood couldn't shake the feeling that he had just crossed an invisible boundary as the door closed behind him. Whatever revelations awaited him here, he sensed they would irrevocably alter the course of his investigation - and perhaps his very understanding of the world.

The parlor enveloped Blackwood in a cocoon of warmth, a stark contrast to the chill that clung to his bones from the foggy streets outside. A fire crackled merrily in the hearth, casting dancing shadows on the floral-patterned wallpaper. The air was perfumed with the comforting aroma of freshly brewed tea, its tendrils of steam curling invitingly from a porcelain pot on a nearby table.

"Please, make yourself comfortable," Agnes said, gesturing to a well-worn armchair that seemed to beckon with the promise of respite.

Blackwood sank into the chair, his body grateful for the reprieve, even as his mind remained razor sharp. He watched Agnes settle across from him, her movements graceful despite her years. Her eyes, keen and knowing, met his with an intensity that belied her gentle demeanor.

"Now then, Detective," she began, leaning forward slightly. "What brings you to my door at this late hour?"

Blackwood took a deep breath, steeling himself. "Mrs. O'Reilly, I'm afraid I come bearing grim news. Professor Algernon Winthrop has been murdered."

Agnes's hand flew to her mouth, her eyes widening. "Good heavens! The poor man. How dreadful!"

"Indeed," Blackwood continued, his voice low and urgent. "But I'm afraid the circumstances of his death are... unusual, to say the least."

As he spoke, detailing the eerie scene he'd encountered and the whispers of supernatural involvement, Blackwood couldn't help but notice the subtle shift in Agnes's expression. Her initial shock gave way to a look of grim understanding, as if pieces of a long-dormant puzzle were falling into place.

"I can see why you've come to me," she murmured, her gaze drifting momentarily to the fire. "You suspect there's more to this than meets the eye, right?"

Blackwood leaned forward, his heart quickening. "You know something of this, don't you, Mrs. O'Reilly? Something beyond the realm of ordinary crime?"

Agnes sighed, a sound heavy with the weight of hidden knowledge. "Oh, my dear boy. There are forces at work in this city that few dare to acknowledge. Dark, ancient things that lurk in the shadows, waiting for their moment to strike."

As she spoke, Blackwood felt a chill run down his spine despite the warmth of the room. He'd always trusted his intuition, that sixth sense that had guided him through countless investigations. Now, it was screaming at him that he stood on the precipice of something far more dangerous than he'd ever encountered.

Agnes's eyes met Blackwood's, her gaze steady and unwavering. She nodded slowly, her silvered hair catching the firelight as she acknowledged the gravity of his words. "The Order of the Eternal Flame," she murmured, her voice barely above a whisper. "I had hoped never to hear that name again."

Blackwood felt his pulse quicken. "You know of them?"

"Oh, love," Agnes sighed, her tone tinged with a mixture of sorrow and apprehension. "I've known of them for longer than I care to admit. They're a shadow that's loomed over this city for centuries, always just out of sight."

As she spoke, Agnes rose from her chair, moving to a small cabinet in the corner of the room. Blackwood watched her, his mind racing with questions. What could this kindly boarding house owner know of such dark matters?

"The Order," Agnes continued, retrieving a worn leather-bound book, "has roots that stretch back to the time of the great plague. They began as seekers of forbidden knowledge, believing they could harness the power of life and death itself."

Blackwood leaned forward, captivated. "And did they succeed?"

Agnes's eyes darkened as she returned to her seat. "In a manner of speaking. But such power always comes at a terrible price, my dear. The practices they delved into... well, let's say they're best left in the shadows where they belong."

As she spoke, Blackwood couldn't help but notice the slight tremor in her hands as she clutched the book. What horrors had this gentle soul witnessed to instill such fear?

Blackwood's piercing blue eyes narrowed, his gaze fixed on the book in Agnes's trembling hands. "And the tome Professor Winthrop was studying?" he pressed, his voice low and urgent. How does it connect to all this?"

Agnes hesitated, her fingers tracing the worn edges of her leather-bound volume. "The tome, dear... it's the key to unlocking the Order's most potent rituals. A compendium of their darkest secrets."

Blackwood felt a chill run down his spine, his mind racing with the implications. He leaned closer, the flickering firelight casting deep shadows across his face. "But why kill for it? What could be so valuable—or dangerous—that it would drive them to murder?"

Agnes's soft voice took on a somber tone.

"Power, love. The kind that corrupts absolutely. It's whispered that the tome contains a ritual to breach the veil between worlds."

Blackwood noticed her gaze drift to the window as she spoke, where the thick London fog pressed against the glass like a living entity.

He followed her line of sight, half-expecting to see ghostly figures materializing in the mist.

"You mean to tell me," Blackwood said, his throat suddenly dry, "that the Order seeks to bring something through from... beyond?"

Agnes nodded gravely, her eyes meeting his with a look of profound concern. "Something ancient and terrible, I fear. And if they succeed, the consequences for our world would be... unthinkable."

Blackwood's mind whirled, the pieces of the puzzle falling into place with alarming clarity.

He rose from his chair, pacing the small parlor as the floorboards creaked beneath his feet.

The crackling fire cast his elongated shadow against the wall, a dark silhouette that seemed to dance with each revelation.

"So, the professor's murder," he mused aloud, his voice tight with tension, "it wasn't just about silencing him. Perhaps they needed something he possessed—a key to deciphering the tome?"

Agnes watched him intently, her weathered hands clasped tightly in her lap. "You've a keen mind, Detective. I believe poor Algernon stumbled upon something the Order desperately wanted to keep hidden."

Blackwood turned to face her, his blue eyes glinting with a mix of determination and barely concealed fear. "And now they have both the tome and whatever secret Winthrop uncovered. We're racing against time, aren't we?"

"Indeed, we are, love," Agnes replied softly, rising to stand beside him. She placed a comforting hand on his arm, her touch grounding him amidst the storm of his thoughts.

"But remember, haste can be as dangerous as hesitation. You must tread carefully, for the Order has eyes and ears everywhere."

Blackwood nodded, feeling the weight of her words settle upon his shoulders. "How do I proceed, Agnes? The fog outside seems less opaque than the path before me."

Agnes's eyes crinkled with a mix of concern and admiration. "Trust your instincts, dear. They've served you well in the past. But above all, guard your mind and your heart. The Order's influence can seep into the most fortified of souls."

Blackwood drew a deep breath, his chest swelling with gratitude for the woman before him. "Agnes, I cannot express how invaluable your guidance has been," he said, his voice low and earnest. "Your wisdom illuminates the path ahead, even as the fog beyond these walls threatens to obscure it."

Agnes's eyes softened, a gentle smile playing at the corners of her mouth. "Oh, love, you've got a heavy burden to bear. I'm just glad I could offer some small comfort."

The Detective's gaze drifted to the window, where tendrils of mist curled against the glass like spectral fingers. His mind whirred with the gravity of the knowledge he'd gained, each revelation a piece in a treacherous puzzle.

"I feel as though I've been given a map," Blackwood mused, half to himself, "but one written in a language I've yet to fully decipher."

He turned back to Agnes, his brow furrowed.

"The Order's reach, the ancient tome, Professor Winthrop's murder - it's all connected. And at the heart of it all, Lady Ravenscroft's restless spirit..."

Agnes nodded solemnly. "Aye, threads in a tapestry woven with blood and shadow."

Blackwood's hand unconsciously moved to his coat pocket, where Lady Ravenscroft's ethereal plea seemed to pulse like a second heartbeat. He felt a renewed sense of purpose course through him, steeling his resolve.

"I cannot falter now," he said, his voice steady despite the tremor in his soul. "Lady Ravenscroft's justice and the safety of countless others depends on unraveling this mystery."

Agnes reached out, patting his hand with motherly affection. "And unravel it, you shall, my dear. Remember, our inner light guides us true in the darkest of nights."

Blackwood rose from his chair, the floorboards creaking softly beneath his feet. Agnes followed suit, her eyes gleaming with concern and admiration. As he reached for his coat, she placed a gentle hand on his arm, her touch as light as a feather yet carrying the weight of centuries.

"Before you go, Arthur," she said, her voice barely above a whisper, "heed this final counsel. Trust the whispers of your heart as much as the deductions of your mind. In the realm of shadows where you tread, intuition may be your most faithful companion."

The Detective paused, absorbing her words.

"My instincts have often led me to truths others overlook," he admitted, his piercing blue eyes meeting her gaze. "Yet the stakes have never been so high."

Agnes nodded, her silver hair catching the firelight. "All the more reason to rely on that inner compass, love. It's guided you this far, hasn't it?"

Blackwood allowed himself a small smile, gratitude warming his usually guarded features.

"Indeed, it has, Mrs. O'Reilly. I shall carry your wisdom with me into the fog."

With a final nod of appreciation, he donned his coat and hat, steeling himself for the chill that awaited beyond the boarding house's welcoming embrace. As he opened the door, a gust of damp air rushed in, carrying the muffled sounds of distant carriages and the acrid scent of coal smoke.

Blackwood stepped out onto the cobblestones, the warmth of Agnes's parlor fading like a half-remembered dream. The fog enveloped him, transforming familiar streets into an otherworldly landscape of shifting shadows and muted echoes.

"Into the heart of the mystery,' he thought, his resolve hardening with each step. 'Where every alley may hide a clue, and every whisper could be a warning."

The Detective's footsteps echoed softly against the damp cobblestones, each resonant tap a reminder of the weighty task before him.

Blackwood pulled his collar up against the chill, his mind racing with the revelations Agnes had shared. The Order of the Eternal Flame, the ancient tome, Professor Winthrop's gruesome fate—all pieces of a puzzle that threatened to consume not just his investigation but the very fabric of London itself.

As he navigated the fogbound streets, Blackwood's keen eyes darted from shadow to shadow, ever vigilant. The gas lamps cast a sickly glow through the mist, their light barely penetrating the gloom that seemed to grow thicker with each passing moment.

"By Jove," he muttered, "what devilry lurks in these shadows?"

A figure emerged from the fog ahead, startling him. Blackwood's hand instinctively moved towards the revolver concealed beneath his coat.

"Evening, guv'nor," the man gasped, revealing himself as nothing more than a chimney sweep making his way home.

Blackwood relaxed, but only slightly. "Good evening," he replied, his voice low and measured.

As the sweep shuffled past, Blackwood's thoughts turned inward. "Every face a potential ally or foe,' he mused. 'Agnes was right—I must trust my instincts now more than ever."

The weight of responsibility pressed down upon him, yet Blackwood felt his determination grow with each step. The darkness threatening London might be formidable, but he was far from powerless. With Agnes's insights and his hard-won experience, he was prepared to pierce the secrecy surrounding the Order.

"Come what may," Blackwood whispered into the night, his words swallowed by the fog, "I shall see justice done."

Chapter 5: Exploration

The fog parted like a ghostly curtain as Detective Arthur Blackwood approached the abandoned mansion, his footsteps echoing hollowly on the worn cobblestones. He paused at the threshold, a chill running down his spine that had nothing to do with the damp night air.

"What secrets do you hold, I wonder?" Arthur murmured, his piercing blue eyes scanning the crumbling facade.

The weight of untold histories seemed to press down upon him, urging caution even as his innate curiosity compelled him forward. Arthur squared his shoulders, steeling himself for what lay ahead. After all, he had faced worse than a decrepit old house in his years as a detective.

With a steadying breath, he grasped the tarnished brass doorknob and pushed. The heavy oak door swung inward with a bone-chilling creak that reverberated through the silent halls. Arthur winced at the sound, half-expecting some otherworldly entity to materialize in response to the intrusion.

"Steady on, old boy," he whispered to himself. "It's only a house, nothing more."

But even as the words left his lips, Arthur knew they rang hollow. This was no ordinary dwelling—it reeked of dark deeds and secrets.

He stepped inside, blinking rapidly as his eyes adjusted to the gloom. Wan beams of moonlight filtered through grimy windows, casting eerie shadows across the entry hall. A thick blanket of dust covered every surface, undisturbed for what must have been decades.

"What happened here?" Arthur mused, his analytical mind already cataloging details.

"And how does it connect to the professor's murder?"

A sudden gust of wind slammed the door shut behind him with a resounding boom. Arthur's hand flew instinctively to the revolver at his hip, his heart racing. The walls seemed to close around him for a moment, whispering forgotten terrors.

He forced himself to breathe slowly, calling upon years of experience with the supernatural to center himself. "There are answers here," Arthur said firmly. "And I intend to find them, come what may."

With that declaration, Detective Blackwood squared his shoulders and ventured deeper into the mansion's shadowy depths, unaware of the ancient eyes that watched his every move from the darkness.

Arthur's keen eyes swept methodically across the entrance hall, his mind cataloging every detail. The faded wallpaper, once richly patterned, now peeled in long strips like decaying skin. Ornate sconces, tarnished with age, stood silent sentinel along the walls. A grand staircase curved upwards into darkness, its balustrade thick with cobwebs.

"Such grandeur," Arthur murmured, his voice barely above a whisper. "Now reduced to this."

His gaze settled on a portrait hanging askew on the far wall. A stern-faced man glowered down at him, his eyes seeming to follow Arthur's movements. The Detective approached, studying the painting intently.

"Who were you, I wonder?" he mused aloud. "A member of the Order, perhaps?"

The portrait offered no answers, but Arthur couldn't shake the feeling of being watched.

He turned away, suppressing a shiver.

"Focus, Blackwood," he scolded himself. "The library. That's where the real answers lie."

With purposeful strides, Arthur made his way deeper into the mansion. The floorboards creaked ominously beneath his feet, each step stirring up clouds of dust. At last, he came upon a set of double doors intricately carved with arcane symbols.

"This must be it," Arthur whispered, pushing the doors open.

The library sprawled before him, a cavernous space filled with towering bookshelves that stretched from floor to ceiling. The air was thick with the musty scent of ancient leather and parchment.

Arthur's heart quickened with anticipation. "If there are answers to be found, surely they're here."

He approached the nearest shelf, running his fingers reverently along the spines of countless tomes. Titles in languages both familiar and utterly foreign met his gaze.

"What secrets did you uncover, Professor Winthrop?" Arthur murmured. "And which of these volumes led you to your doom?"

As he searched, Arthur couldn't shake the feeling that the very walls were listening, waiting with bated breath to see what he might discover in this sanctum of forgotten knowledge.

Arthur's keen eyes scanned the shelves, his mind racing to connect the disparate threads of the investigation. Suddenly, his fingers brushed against a book that seemed oddly out of place. With a soft click, a hidden compartment sprang open behind the row of books, revealing a cache of yellowed documents and peculiar artifacts.

"By Jove," Arthur breathed, his heart pounding. "What have we here?"

Carefully, he extracted the items and laid them out on a nearby desk. His brow furrowed as he examined each piece, recognizing symbols that had haunted his dreams since he first encountered the Order of the Eternal Flame.

"These markings," he muttered, tracing a finger over an intricate diagram. "The same as those found at the scene of Professor Winthrop's murder."

A chill ran down his spine as Arthur delved deeper into the documents. The air around him seemed to thicken, and he could have sworn he heard a faint whispering as if the walls were trying to communicate.

"Steady on, Blackwood," he told himself, fighting to maintain his composure. "You've faced worse than disembodied voices."

The whispers grew more insistent, but Arthur forced himself to focus on the task. His eyes narrowed as he deciphered a particularly cryptic passage.

"The flame that never dies," he read aloud, his voice barely above a whisper. "What secrets do you guard, I wonder?"

As he spoke, the whispering seemed to intensify, growing more urgent. Arthur's hand instinctively moved to the revolver at his hip, even as he continued to study the documents.

"I won't be deterred," he said firmly, as much to himself as to the unseen presence he sensed around him. "These secrets have already cost one life. I intend to see justice done, no matter the cost."

With renewed determination, Arthur bent over the papers, his mind racing to unravel the mystery that had brought him to this foreboding mansion. The whispering faded to a dull murmur, but the weight of unseen eyes upon him remained, a constant reminder of the dangers lurking in Victorian London's shadows.

Arthur's piercing blue eyes darted across the scattered papers, his brow furrowing as he absorbed each detail. Suddenly, a peculiar map caught his attention, its edges worn and yellowed with age.

"What have we here?" he murmured, carefully unfolding the parchment. Locations were marked with an intricate symbol—a flame encircled by thorns. "The Order's handiwork, no doubt."

He traced the markings with a calloused finger, committing each to memory. The fog seemed to press against the windows, eager to witness his discovery.

"These locations," Arthur mused aloud, his voice low and measured. "They form a pattern. But to what end?"

As he studied the map, a chill ran down his spine. The whispers from earlier had returned, now a barely audible hum that seemed to emanate from the walls.

Shaking off the eerie sensation, Arthur focused on the task at hand. "I must remember every detail. This could be the key to unraveling the whole sordid affair."

With a final, scrutinizing glance, he carefully refolded the map and tucked it into his coat pocket. As he turned to continue his exploration, a floorboard creaked beneath his feet, revealing the edge of a concealed door.

"Well, well," Arthur murmured, a mixture of trepidation and excitement coloring his tone.

"What other secrets do you hold, old house?"

He hesitated for a moment, hand hovering over the hidden latch. The whispers grew more insistent, almost warning in their tone. Arthur steeled himself, memories of past supernatural encounters flashing through his mind.

"I've come too far to turn back now," he declared, his voice steady despite the rapid beating of his heart.

With a deep breath, he pulled the latch. The concealed door swung open with a groan, revealing a narrow staircase descending into impenetrable darkness. The damp, musty air that wafted up seemed to carry the weight of centuries.

Arthur paused at the threshold, peering into the gloom. "Into the belly of the beast," he muttered, reaching for his lantern. With a final glance over his shoulder at the relative safety of the library, he began his descent.

Each step echoed ominously in the confined space, the sound rebounding off unseen walls.

The darkness seemed to press in around him, held at bay only by the feeble light of his lantern.

"What lies at the bottom, I wonder?" Arthur mused aloud, his words barely audible over the pounding of his own heart. "The answers I seek, or merely more questions?"

As he continued downward, the whispers from above faded, replaced by an oppressive silence that seemed to watch his every move with evil intent.

As Arthur reached the bottom of the staircase, the narrow passage opened into a vast chamber, its true dimensions obscured by the dim light. His lantern flickered, casting eerie shadows across walls adorned with strange, arcane symbols etched deep into the stone.

"Good Lord," he whispered, his voice barely audible in the oppressive silence. The air hung thick and heavy, charged with an inexplicable energy that made the hairs on the back of his neck stand on end.

Arthur's keen eyes swept across the chamber, taking in every detail. The symbols seemed to writhe and dance in the wavering lantern light, their meanings just beyond the grasp of comprehension. He stepped forward, his footfalls echoing ominously.

"What manner of place is this?" he mused aloud, his words swallowed by the vastness of the chamber. "These symbols... they're unlike anything I've encountered before."

As he moved deeper into the room, the center came into focus. An altar stood, bathed in a shaft of pale light from an unseen source. Its surface was adorned with objects that sent a chill down Arthur's spine.

"So, the Order's tendrils reach even here," he muttered, approaching the altar cautiously.

"But to what end?"

Arthur's trained eye cataloged the items before him: a silver chalice encrusted with dark gemstones, a dagger with an intricately carved bone handle, and a leather-bound tome whose very presence seemed to emanate malevolence.

He reached out, his fingers hovering over the dagger. "Each piece is a key to unlocking this infernal puzzle," he said, his voice tinged with fascination and disgust. But at what cost to those who seek such knowledge?"

Arthur tried to understand how the mansion, the Order, and Professor Winthrop's deaths were related. The weight of the investigation pressed down upon him, as tangible as the suffocating air of the chamber.

"What dark rituals were performed here?" he wondered aloud, his gaze sweeping the symbols again. "And how does it all tie back to Winthrop's murder?"

A sudden chill swept through the chamber as Arthur's fingers grazed the altar's surface. The air around him seemed to thicken, and the hairs on his neck stood on end. He froze, his senses heightened to an almost painful degree.

"I am not alone," he whispered, his breath misting in the frigid air.

Years of confronting the supernatural had honed Arthur's instincts, and now they screamed of an unseen presence. He closed his eyes, drawing upon the reserves of calm he had cultivated through countless harrowing encounters.

"Show yourself," he commanded, his voice steady despite his heart racing. "Or are you content to lurk in the shadows, watching?"

Silence answered him, but the feeling of being observed intensified. Arthur's mind raced, recalling similar experiences from past cases.

He opened his eyes, scanning the room methodically.

"Very well," he murmured. "Keep your secrets for now. But know this—I will uncover the truth, no matter the cost."

A faint whisper of movement caught his attention, as if in response to his declaration.

Arthur's gaze snapped to a far corner of the chamber, where a tattered tapestry stirred ever so slightly.

"Ah," he said, a grim smile on his lips. "What have we here?"

With measured steps, Arthur approached the tapestry. Its faded threads depicted a scene of arcane rituals, figures cloaked in shadow performing acts that made even his seasoned stomach turn. He reached out, running his fingers along the edge of the heavy fabric.

"The Order's secrets run deep," he mused, "but not deep enough to escape my notice."

With a swift motion, Arthur pulled the tapestry aside, revealing a narrow passageway hewn into the stone. A draft of stale air wafted from the opening, carrying the musty scent of age and forgotten secrets.

"Into the belly of the beast," Arthur muttered, steeling himself for what lay ahead. "Whatever truths you hide, mansion, I will drag them into the light."

Without hesitation, he stepped into the passageway, the weight of his responsibility to solve Winthrop's murder driving him forward into the unknown depths of the mansion's secrets.

Arthur emerged from the hidden passage, his eyes widening as he beheld the grand ballroom. The once-opulent chamber stretched in faded grandeur, its gilded mirrors tarnished and cracked, dusty crystal chandeliers hanging precariously from the vaulted ceiling.

"By Jove," he whispered, his voice echoing in the cavernous space. "What secrets have you witnessed, I wonder?"

As he stepped further into the room, the floorboards creaked beneath his feet, releasing puffs of dust that danced in the dim light filtering through grimy windows. Arthur's keen gaze swept across the room, cataloging every detail.

His attention was drawn to a large painting adorning one wall, its subject a stern-faced man in ornate robes. "Could it be?" Arthur mused aloud, approaching the portrait. "The founder of the Order himself?"

The Detective's mind raced, connecting threads of information. "The symbols in the chamber below, the ritualistic objects, and now this... The Order's influence runs deeper than I imagined."

A glint of metal caught his eye, and Arthur knelt to examine a small object half-hidden beneath a rotting curtain. "What have we here?" He carefully extracted a medallion, its surface etched with familiar symbols. "Another piece of the puzzle, no doubt."

As he stood, a sudden chill ran down Arthur's spine. The weight of his discoveries pressed upon him, and he could almost feel the mansion's secrets swirling around him like a palpable force.

"I must leave this place," he muttered, pocketing the medallion. "But not before one last look."

Arthur's gaze swept the ballroom again, his mind cataloging every detail. "The Order, the mansion, Winthrop's murder... They're all connected, I'm certain of it."

He paused at the threshold, a determined set to his jaw. Whatever dark forces are at play," he vowed, "I will unravel this mystery—for you, Winthrop, and for all those who may fall victim to the Order's machinations."

With a final, resolute nod, Arthur turned to leave the mansion. His discoveries were heavy on his shoulders, but his progress buoyed his spirit. The true investigation, he knew, was only beginning.

Arthur Blackwood stepped out of the mansion, the heavy door groaning shut behind him with an ominous finality. The fog-laden streets of London enveloped him, a thick, spectral veil that seemed to pulse with secrets. He paused on the threshold, his piercing blue eyes scanning the murky surroundings.

"By God," he muttered, his breath visible in the chill air, "it's as if the very mists conspire to conceal the truth."

As he descended the crumbling steps, Arthur's mind raced with the implications of his discoveries. The weight of the medallion in his pocket seemed to grow heavier with each step.

"The Order's reach extends far beyond what we initially surmised," he mused, his voice barely above a whisper. "But to what end? And how does Winthrop's research factor into their grand design?"

A nearby gas lamp flickered, casting elongated shadows that danced across the cobblestones.

Arthur instinctively tensed, his hand moving to the revolver concealed beneath his coat.

He thought I'd dealt with otherworldly threats before, but this feels different. The Order's influence permeates the very fabric of our city.

"I must proceed with utmost caution," Arthur said, his tone resolute. "The answers lie within the shadows of the past, and I shall drag them into the light, no matter the cost."

As he strode purposefully into the fog-shrouded street, the Detective's mind whirred with possibilities. The clues he had uncovered in the mansion were pieces of a larger, more sinister puzzle.

"Winthrop, old friend," he murmured, his voice tinged with sorrow and determination. I swear I shall uncover the truth behind your murder. The Order may lurk in darkness, but they shall soon learn that I am quite adept at navigating the gloom."

Chapter 6: First Challenge

The rusted gates groaned in protest as Detective Arthur Blackwood pushed them aside, revealing the decaying grandeur of Ravenscroft Manor. Beside him, Lady Eleanor Ravenscroft's spectral form shimmered, her ethereal glow casting long shadows across the overgrown path.

"We must tread carefully, my lady," Blackwood whispered, his piercing blue eyes scanning the crumbling facade. "This place harbors secrets best left undisturbed."

Lady Ravenscroft's voice carried on a ghostly breeze. "Yet disturb them we must, Detective. The truth cannot remain buried forever."

Blackwood nodded grimly, steeling himself against the chill that seeped into his bones. The weight of unsolved mysteries pressed upon him, driving him forward despite the mansion's foreboding aura. As they crossed the threshold, the floorboards creaked ominously underfoot.

The Detective's nostrils flared, assaulted by the musty odor of decay and neglect. Dust motes danced in the faint moonlight filtering through grimy windows, painting macabre patterns on peeling wallpaper. Each step echoed hollowly through the desolate halls, a grim reminder of the lives once lived—and perhaps lost—within these walls.

"The air itself seems thick with sorrow," Blackwood mused, his voice barely above a whisper. "What tragedies have these walls witnessed, I wonder?"

Lady Ravenscroft's form flickered, her spectral visage etched with centuries of pain. "More than you can imagine, Detective. But we cannot dwell on past sorrows. Our path lies ahead."

Blackwood's keen instincts prickled as they delved deeper into the mansion's labyrinthine corridors. The oppressive darkness seemed to close in around them, held at bay only by Lady Ravenscroft's soft luminescence. He found himself grateful for her presence, a beacon of otherworldly comfort in this realm of shadows.

"Your intuition has served us well thus far," Lady Ravenscroft observed. "What does it tell you now?"

Blackwood paused, letting his senses attune to the mansion's eerie stillness. "There's a pull," he murmured, "drawing us downward. The vault we seek lies in the bowels of this place; I'm certain of it."

As they descended a narrow staircase, the Detective's mind raced. What secrets lay hidden in the depths of Ravenscroft Manor?

And more importantly, what price would they pay to uncover them? The weight of responsibility settled heavily upon his shoulders.

Still, Blackwood pressed on, driven by an unwavering commitment to justice—both for the living and the dead.

The massive vault door loomed before them, its intricate metalwork a testament to the craftsmen of a bygone era. Blackwood approached with reverence, his fingers hovering just above the surface before making contact with the cold steel.

"Remarkable," he breathed, tracing the elaborate patterns etched into the lock mechanism. "This is no ordinary vault, Lady Ravenscroft. The complexity... it's as if it was designed to keep something in, rather than merely keeping intruders out."

As he spoke, Blackwood's practiced hands explored every contour and crevice of the lock. His brow furrowed in concentration, and his blue eyes narrowed as he cataloged each detail.

"What do you sense, Detective?" Lady Ravenscroft's ethereal voice floated beside him.

Blackwood paused, his palm flat against the door. "There's a weight here, my Lady. Not just physical, but... spiritual. As if the knowledge contained within presses against the other side, yearning to be free." He turned to face her, his expression grave. "The answers we seek are here, I'm certain. But I fear they may come at a terrible cost."

Lady Ravenscroft nodded solemnly.

"Knowledge always does, Arthur. But we've come too far to turn back now."

She glided forward, her spectral form shimmering in the gloom. As she extended her hand toward the lock, Blackwood felt the air around them change, charged with an otherworldly energy that made the hairs on the back of his neck stand on end.

"What are you—" he began but fell silent as Lady Ravenscroft's fingers brushed against the metal.

A soft blue glow emanated from her touch, seeping into the lock's intricate workings. The tumblers within began to shift and click, a sound that reverberated through the cavernous space with unnatural clarity.

Blackwood watched in awe, his analytical mind struggling to reconcile the supernatural event unfolding before him. "Extraordinary," he whispered. "Your connection to this place, the very fabric of the unseen world... it's unlike anything I've encountered."

Lady Ravenscroft withdrew her hand as the final tumbler fell into place with a resounding click. "The way is open, Detective," she said, her voice tinged with triumph and trepidation. "Are you prepared for what lies beyond?"

Blackwood squared his shoulders, steeling himself for whatever revelations awaited. "As prepared as one can be when treading the line between the known and the unknowable, my Lady. Shall we?"

The ancient hinges groaned in protest as the vault door swung open, unleashing a gust of frigid air that carried with it the musty scent of centuries past. Blackwood instinctively raised an arm to shield his face, his keen eyes narrowing against the sudden chill.

"By God," he breathed, lowering his arm as the initial rush subsided. "Can you hear them, Lady Ravenscroft? The whispers?"

Indeed, barely audible beneath the creak of the door, a cacophony of faint, unintelligible murmurs seemed to emanate from the darkness beyond. Lady Ravenscroft's ethereal form shimmered her expression a mixture of determination and apprehension.

"I hear them, Detective," she replied, her voice carrying the weight of centuries. "The voices of forgotten souls, perhaps? Or something far more sinister?"

Blackwood's hand instinctively moved to the revolver holstered at his side. "Whatever the source, we must press on. The answers we seek lie within." He paused, turning to face his spectral companion. "My Lady, I confess I find myself grateful for your presence. Your... unique abilities may prove invaluable in navigating what lies ahead."

Lady Ravenscroft's lips curved into a sad smile.

"As am I for yours, Detective. The realms of the living and the dead intertwine here. We shall need each other's strengths."

With a nod of agreement, Blackwood stepped into the vault's yawning darkness. Lady Ravenscroft glided beside him, her faint luminescence casting eerie shadows across the chamber's interior.

As Blackwood's eyes adjusted to the gloom, he found himself surrounded by towering shelves laden with ancient tomes and artifacts. The air was thick with dust and the unmistakable odor of decay. His gaze darted from object to object, his mind racing to catalog each potential clue.

"Good Lord," he muttered, brushing his fingers along the spine of a particularly ominous-looking volume. "The knowledge contained here... it's staggering. And dangerous, no doubt."

Lady Ravenscroft drifted towards a collection of peculiar relics arranged on a nearby table.

"Indeed, Detective. I sense great power here but also great malevolence. We must tread carefully."

Blackwood nodded, his brow furrowed in concentration. "The Order's secrets are here, hidden among these arcane treasures. But where to begin? What thread will unravel their sinister plot?"

His eyes fell upon a small, ornate box tucked away on a lower shelf as he spoke. Something about it called to him a feeling he had learned to trust over his years of investigating the unexplainable.

"Lady Ravenscroft," he said, kneeling to examine the box more closely, "I believe I may have found our first clue. What do you make of this?"

A sudden chill permeated the air as Blackwood's fingers brushed the ornate box, misting his breath. The shadows in the corners of the vault seemed to deepen, coalescing into a swirling mass of darkness that materialized between them and their prize.

Blackwood recoiled, his heart racing as an oppressive weight settled upon him. The wraith's form undulated, its very presence a palpable malevolence that sent icy tendrils of fear down his spine.

"By all that's holy," he whispered, his voice barely audible over his thundering pulse. The Detective's mind raced, recalling every encounter with the supernatural he'd ever faced. Yet, nothing had prepared him for this guardian of forbidden knowledge.

Lady Ravenscroft's ethereal form shimmered, her spectral light intensifying as she positioned herself between Blackwood and the menacing apparition. Her voice, though soft, resonated with an otherworldly authority that filled the chamber.

"You have no dominion here, shade," she declared, her translucent form growing more substantial with each word. "We seek truths long hidden, and your presence shall not deter us from our righteous path."

Blackwood marveled at his companion's courage, even as he fought to master his fear.

He thought, "Her strength is remarkable, but will it be enough against such malice incarnate?"

The wraith's form writhed in response to Lady Ravenscroft's challenge, its voiceless fury palpable in the frigid air. Blackwood steeled himself, ready to face whatever onslaught might come, his resolve strengthened by the Lady's unwavering defiance.

The wraith's form coalesced into a mass of writhing shadows, its tendrils lashing out with preternatural speed towards Blackwood. The Detective's instincts, honed by years of supernatural encounters, took over. He dove to the side, rolling across the cold stone floor and coming up in a defensive crouch.

"Lady Ravenscroft!" Blackwood called out, his voice tight with tension. "Its form—it's not entirely corporeal. We must find a way to disrupt its cohesion!"

As he spoke, Blackwood's mind raced through his repertoire of arcane knowledge. 'Salt, iron, or perhaps a binding incantation?' he pondered, his eyes darting around the vault for anything that might serve as a weapon.

Lady Ravenscroft's spectral form flickered, her essence merging with the air around them.

"Arthur," her voice echoed, carrying an otherworldly resonance, "your mortal strength combined with my ethereal nature may be our key. We must act as one!"

Blackwood nodded, understanding dawning in his eyes. He moved with deliberate grace, positioning himself back-to-back with Lady Ravenscroft's luminous form. The wraith circled them, its malevolent presence a constant pressure against their senses.

"On my mark," Blackwood murmured, his muscles taut with anticipation. He felt Lady Ravenscroft's spectral energy pulsing behind him, a comforting warmth against the chill of the vault.

The wraith lunged once more, its dark tendrils reaching for them both. Blackwood's voice rang out, "Now!"

In perfect synchronization, Blackwood ducked as Lady Ravenscroft's form expanded, her spectral light intensifying to a brilliant radiance.

The Detective's hands, guided by an intuition he couldn't explain, moved through the air, tracing arcane symbols that seemed to draw power from Lady Ravenscroft's essence.

'This connection,' Blackwood marveled inwardly, "unlike anything I've experienced. Our very essences intertwined against this abomination."

The wraith's form convulsed, its inky tendrils recoiling from the combined assault of mortal and spirit. Blackwood pressed forward, his movements fluid and purposeful, each gesture a defiance against the supernatural malevolence before them.

"We're weakening it, Arthur!" Lady Ravenscroft's voice resonated with a mix of exhilaration and strain. "But we must not falter!"

Blackwood gritted his teeth, perspiration beading on his brow. "Indeed, my Lady. This creature guards secrets we must uncover, no matter the cost."

The Detective's mind raced, recalling fragments of lore from past encounters. "The wraith's essence flickers like a candle in a storm. Perhaps..."

"Lady Ravenscroft," he called out, his voice steady despite the exertion, "can you draw its attention? I believe I see a vulnerability."

The spectral noblewoman's form shimmered, her ethereal light pulsing brighter. "Consider it done, dear Arthur. But make haste—even I have limits in this form."

As Lady Ravenscroft engaged the wraith in a dazzling display of spectral energy, Blackwood circled behind, his eyes fixed on a pulsating core within the creature's shadowy mass. With a sharp intake of breath, he plunged his hand into the writhing darkness.

"By all that's holy," he gasped, the cold of the void seeping into his very bones, "I banish thee!"

The wraith let out an unearthly shriek, its form collapsing in on itself. Blackwood stumbled backward, his breath coming in ragged gasps as he watched the creature dissipate into wisps of shadow.

The oppressive silence that followed the wraith's demise was broken only by Blackwood's labored breathing. His piercing blue eyes, now tinged with exhaustion, scanned the vault's gloomy interior. Dust motes danced in the faint, ethereal light emanating from Lady Ravenscroft's spectral form.

"My lady," Blackwood began, his voice hoarse but filled with genuine admiration, "your assistance was... invaluable. I fear I would have fared poorly against such a foe alone."

Lady Ravenscroft's translucent features softened, a smile playing at the corners of her otherworldly visage. "You sell yourself short, Arthur. Your intuition and courage are formidable weapons in their own right."

Blackwood allowed himself a small nod of acknowledgment, his mind already racing ahead to the task at hand. "The secrets contained within these walls,' he mused, 'what dark truths do they hold?"

"We mustn't dawdle," he said aloud, moving towards a nearby bookshelf laden with ancient tomes. "Professor Winthrop's research... it must be here somewhere."

Lady Ravenscroft glided to a dusty writing desk, her spectral fingers hovering over scattered papers. "Indeed. The Order's machinations run deep, Arthur. I sense a malevolence here that chills even my incorporeal form."

As Blackwood carefully extracted a leather-bound journal from the shelf, he felt a familiar tingle at the base of his skull—an instinct honed by years of supernatural encounters. "Tell me, my lady," he said, his voice low and measured, "what do your otherworldly senses perceive?"

The ghostly noblewoman closed her eyes, her form shimmering like a mirage. "Echoes of dark rituals, Arthur. Whispers of power and corruption have seeped into this place's very stones."

Blackwood's fingers trembled slightly as he opened the journal, its pages yellowed with age. "Then we must be prepared for whatever horrors these documents may reveal. The Order's reach seems to extend beyond the grave itself."

As they delved deeper into the vault's contents, each revelation brought a mix of dread and grim determination. Blackwood's detective mind worked feverishly, connecting fragments of information like pieces of a macabre puzzle.

"By God," he muttered, his eyes widening as he deciphered a particularly cryptic passage, "the Order's ambitions... they seek to breach the barriers between worlds."

Lady Ravenscroft's ethereal form flickered with concern. "To what end, Arthur? Surely, they must know the dangers of such meddling."

Blackwood's jaw clenched, his voice barely above a whisper. "Power, my Lady. Unbridled and unchecked. And if we fail to stop them, I fear the consequences will be... unimaginable."

Blackwood's hand rested on the cold iron handle of the vault door, his fingers tracing the intricate engravings as he paused at the threshold. The weight of their discoveries pressed upon him like a physical burden, each revelation a link in a chain that bound him ever tighter to this perilous quest.

"We cannot linger here," he murmured, his piercing blue eyes scanning the shadowy recesses of the vault one last time. "The Order's agents may already be on our trail."

Lady Ravenscroft's spectral form drifted closer, her ethereal presence a stark contrast to the oppressive gloom. "You seem troubled, Arthur. More so than usual."

Blackwood's lips tightened into a grim line. "It's the magnitude of what we face, Eleanor. The Order's reach, their ambitions... it's far beyond anything I've encountered before."

He turned to face her, his expression a mixture of determination and vulnerability. "I find myself questioning whether I'm truly equipped to confront such malevolence."

"Doubt is a luxury we cannot afford," Lady Ravenscroft replied, carrying centuries of wisdom. "Your resolve has brought us this far and will see us through."

Blackwood nodded, drawing strength from her words. His mind raced with possibilities and dangers as they made their way through the mansion's decaying corridors.

"We must tread carefully," he said, his voice barely above a whisper. "Every shadow could conceal an enemy, every whisper a trap."

Lady Ravenscroft's form shimmered with agreement. "Indeed. But remember, Arthur, you do not face this alone. Our bond, forged in the crucible of shared peril, is a formidable weapon."

As they approached the mansion's entrance, Blackwood paused, his hand instinctively reaching for the revolver concealed beneath his coat. The fog outside seemed to press against the windows, an impenetrable veil that could hide untold dangers.

"Whatever lies ahead," he said, his voice filled with quiet resolve, "we will face it together. The Order may have centuries of dark knowledge at their disposal, but they underestimate the power of a righteous cause."

With a deep breath, Blackwood pushed open the heavy oak door, ready to step once more into the fogbound streets of London, where every shadow held the potential for both allies and enemies.

Chapter 7: Gathering Allies

The heavy oak door creaked open, admitting a gust of fog-laden air that swirled around Detective Arthur Blackwood's feet as he stepped into the dimly lit café. Gas lamps flickered weakly, casting dancing shadows across weathered tables and hunched figures engaged in hushed discourse. The rich aroma of freshly ground coffee mingled with the acrid scent of tobacco smoke, creating an atmosphere thick with secrecy.

Blackwood's piercing blue eyes swept the room, seeking his quarry amidst the sea of bowler hats and high collars. There, in the farthest corner, a flash of auburn hair caught his attention. Evelyn Bradshaw sat alone, her back to the wall, a steaming cup cradled in her gloved hands.

Blackwood's mind raced as he wound his way through the cramped space. "What new lead has she uncovered?" he pondered. "And at what risk to herself?" His respect for the intrepid journalist had grown with each encounter, though he couldn't shake a gnawing concern for her safety.

Reaching the table, Blackwood offered a curt nod. "Miss Bradshaw," he murmured, his voice low and measured.

Evelyn's gaze met his, and she had a glimmer of satisfaction in her eyes. "Detective," she replied, gesturing to the empty chair. I trust you weren't followed."

"I took every precaution," Blackwood assured her, settling into the seat. He leaned forward, his elbows on the table. "Your message was rather cryptic. What have you discovered?"

A wry smile played at the corners of Evelyn's lips. "Patience, Detective. Even these walls may have ears."

Blackwood's brow furrowed, his intuition prickling. Whatever Evelyn had uncovered was clearly of great import—and potentially dangerous. He watched as she reached into her reticule, withdrawing a folded piece of paper.

"Before I show you this," Evelyn whispered, her fingers tracing the edge of the document, "I need your word that we're in this together. No lone heroics, no keeping me in the dark. We're partners in this investigation."

Blackwood hesitated, weighing his response. His instinct was to protect her, to shield her from the horrors he'd witnessed. And yet, her tenacity and insight had proven invaluable. He nodded slowly. "You have my word, Miss Bradshaw. Now, what have you found?"

Evelyn's eyes gleamed triumph and trepidation as she unfolded the paper, sliding it across the table. "The Order of the Eternal Flame," she began, her voice low but thrumming with excitement. They're not merely a group of eccentric occultists, Detective. They're far more organized—and dangerous—than we initially believed."

Blackwood leaned in, his gaze fixed on Evelyn's face as she spoke. The cafe's dim light cast shadows across her features, accentuating the determination etched in every line.

"I've traced their origins back to the 17th century," Evelyn continued her words precise and measured. "They began as a secret society within the Royal Society, dabbling in alchemy and what they called 'natural magic.' But over time, their pursuits... darkened."

As she spoke, Blackwood was captivated not just by her words but also by the keen intelligence behind them. Her research was meticulous, her deductions razor-sharp. He felt a grudging admiration growing within him, tempered by a nagging worry about the depths she was willing to plumb for the truth.

"And now?" Blackwood prompted, his voice barely above a whisper.

Evelyn leaned closer, her eyes alight with the thrill of discovery. "Now, they seek something beyond mere knowledge. They believe they've found a way to harness otherworldly powers, to bend the very fabric of reality to their will."

Blackwood suppressed a shudder, memories of past encounters with the supernatural flashing through his mind. He kept his face impassive, but his thoughts raced. If Evelyn was right—and his instincts told him she was—they faced a more significant threat than he'd imagined.

"You've done remarkable work, Miss Bradshaw," he murmured with genuine admiration. "But I fear you may have placed yourself in grave danger."

Evelyn's chin lifted, defiance flashing in her eyes. "Danger is my stock in trade, Detective. As it is yours. The question is, what do we do with this information?"

Evelyn's hand disappeared into her satchel, emerging with a yellowed envelope. "This, Detective Blackwood, is why I asked you here."

She slid the letter across the table, her fingers lingering on its edge.

Blackwood leaned forward, his piercing blue eyes narrowing as he examined the faded script. The letter bore no address, only an intricate seal of a flame encircled by a serpent.

His pulse quickened as he gently unfolded the brittle paper.

"Where did you obtain this?" he asked, his voice low and tense.

"Let's just say I have my sources," Evelyn replied with a hint of smugness. "What matters is its contents."

As Blackwood's eyes scanned the cryptic text, his brow furrowed. Phrases leapt out at him: "convergence of the spheres," "the veil grows thin, sacrifice at the appointed hour." A chill crept up his spine, memories of past encounters with the supernatural stirring in the recesses of his mind.

"This speaks of a ritual," he muttered, more to himself than to Evelyn.

"Something...unprecedented."

Evelyn nodded eagerly. "Exactly. But what kind of ritual? And to what end?"

Blackwood's mind raced, piecing together fragments of information from past cases. "In my experience," he began, choosing his words carefully, "such groups often seek to breach the boundaries between our world and...others. But the scale of this..." He trailed off, lost in thought.

"You've encountered similar cases before?" Evelyn pressed, leaning in closer.

Blackwood met her gaze, weighing how much to reveal. "I have," he admitted. "Though nothing quite like this. The Order of the Eternal Flame seems to be operating on a level far beyond the occult dabblers I've dealt with in the past."

He paused, studying Evelyn's reaction. Her eyes were bright with curiosity, but he detected no fear. It both impressed and concerned him.

"Miss Bradshaw," he continued in a grave tone, "I cannot stress enough the danger we may be facing. The forces these people seek to manipulate are not to be trifled with. I've seen the consequences of such meddling, and they are...dire."

Evelyn's expression hardened with determination. "All the more reason to stop them, wouldn't you agree?"

Blackwood nodded slowly, a reluctant smile tugging at the corners of his mouth. "Indeed. Though it will require utmost caution. And... collaboration." He extended his hand across the table. "I believe our skills may complement each other in this investigation."

As Evelyn's hand met his in a firm shake, Blackwood couldn't shake the feeling that they were embarking on a journey that would test them both to their limits.

The handshake lingered longer than necessary, silently acknowledging their newfound alliance.

As they withdrew, Blackwood noticed a flicker of something in Evelyn's eyes—respect, perhaps, or a hint of relief at not facing this daunting task alone.

"Now, Miss Bradshaw," he said, his voice low and measured, "tell me more about your theories regarding the Order's obsession with the occult."

Evelyn's posture straightened, her hands clasping together on the table as she leaned forward. "From what I've uncovered, Detective, the Order believes in harnessing otherworldly energies for their gain. They speak of ancient rituals and forgotten gods, but it's more than mere superstition."

Blackwood's brow furrowed, his mind racing to connect this information with his experiences.

"How so?" he prompted, his piercing blue eyes fixed on her face.

"Their practices," Evelyn continued, her voice barely above a whisper, "seem to yield... results.

Unexplainable occurrences, witnesses reporting strange phenomena. I've interviewed individuals who claim to have seen Order members perform feats that defy natural law."

Blackwood nodded slowly, his fingers drumming a thoughtful rhythm on the table. "I've encountered similar manifestations in past cases," he mused, more to himself than to Evelyn. "But never on this scale. What do you believe their ultimate goal to be?"

As Evelyn launched her response, Blackwood was impressed by her astute observations and logical deductions. While potentially dangerous, her fearless curiosity proved to be an invaluable asset. He listened intently, occasionally interjecting with questions that probed deeper into the heart of the matter.

"And the sacrificial elements you mentioned earlier," he said, leaning in closer, "how do they fit into this grand design?"

A shadow passed over Evelyn's face. "That's where it becomes truly sinister, Detective. The Order seems to believe that certain rituals require... a price to be paid. In blood."

Blackwood felt a chill run down his spine, memories of past horrors threatening to surface.

He pushed them aside, focusing on the task at hand. "We must tread carefully, Miss Bradshaw. The depths of human depravity in service of such misguided beliefs can be... limitless."

Blackwood found himself increasingly grateful for Evelyn's presence as their discussion continued. Her sharp mind and unwavering determination complemented his own methodical approach. Together, he realized, they stood a far greater chance of unraveling this dark mystery and bringing the Order to justice.

Evelyn's eyes suddenly lit up with a fierce intensity. She leaned forward, her voice dropping to an urgent whisper. "Detective Blackwood, I've uncovered something crucial.

A location tied to the Order's clandestine meetings."

Blackwood's eyes narrowed, his entire demeanor sharpening with keen interest.

"Where?" he asked, his voice low and measured.

"An abandoned chapel on the outskirts of Whitechapel," Evelyn replied, her words tumbling out in a rush of excitement. "It's been boarded up for years, but I've observed suspicious activity there during the witching hour."

Blackwood's mind raced, connecting this new piece of information with the tapestry of clues they'd been weaving. "A forsaken house of worship," he mused, his piercing blue eyes distant. "How fitting for their blasphemous rites."

"Exactly," Evelyn nodded eagerly. "We must investigate it, and soon. Who knows what dark ceremonies they might be planning?"

Blackwood held up a cautionary hand.

"Patience, Miss Bradshaw. We cannot rush headlong into danger without proper preparation."

Evelyn's brow furrowed, a flicker of frustration crossing her face. "But every moment we delay—"

"—is a moment we can use to our advantage," Blackwood finished, his tone firm but not unkind.

"Your intrepid spirit is admirable, but we must approach this methodically."

As they began to strategize, Blackwood appreciated the balance Evelyn brought to their partnership. Her fearless curiosity pushed him to consider bolder moves, while his cautious approach tempered her more impulsive instincts.

"We'll need to observe the chapel first," Blackwood said, outlining his thoughts. "Establish patterns, identify key players. Only then can we plan our next move effectively."

Evelyn nodded, her initial impatience giving way to understanding. "You're right, of course. I can use my contacts in the area to gather initial intelligence without arousing suspicion."

"Excellent," Blackwood replied, a hint of a smile tugging at his lips. "Meanwhile, I'll delve into the historical records of the chapel. There may be architectural details or hidden passages we can exploit."

As they continued to plan, Blackwood felt a growing sense of purpose. Together, they forged a formidable alliance against the darkness that threatened to engulf London. Yet beneath his composed exterior, a nagging worry persisted. The closer they drew to the heart of this conspiracy, the greater the danger awaited them in their beloved city's fog-shrouded streets.

Blackwood rose from his seat, the legs of his chair scraping softly against the worn wooden floor. He offered Evelyn a reassuring nod, his piercing blue eyes meeting hers with a silent understanding. "We've no time to waste, Miss Bradshaw. Shall we?"

Evelyn stood, smoothing her skirts with a determined flourish. "Indeed, Detective. The Order won't unravel itself."

As they made their way to the café's exit, Blackwood's mind raced with possibilities, each step bringing them closer to the unknown dangers that lay ahead. He held the door open for Evelyn, and together, they stepped out into the embrace of London's fog-laden streets.

The transformation was immediate and disorienting. The warm, close air of the café gave way to a chill that seeped through their clothing, carrying with it the acrid scent of coal smoke. Blackwood instinctively pulled his coat tighter around him, his eyes straining to pierce the veil of mist that shrouded the world beyond arm's reach.

"It's as if the very air conspires to keep the city's secrets," Evelyn murmured, her breath forming ghostly wisps in the cold.

Blackwood nodded grimly. "And yet, we must be the ones to uncover them."

They set off down the cobblestone street, their footsteps echoing in the eerie silence. Gas lamps flickered weakly through the fog, casting distorted shadows that danced and writhed along the brick facades of the buildings.

Blackwood found himself hyper-aware of every sound, every movement in the gloom.

"Tell me, Miss Bradshaw," he said softly, his voice barely above a whisper, "do you believe in fate? Perhaps we were meant to unravel this mystery together?"

Evelyn's reply came with a hint of amusement. "I believe in making our fate, Detective. But I won't deny there's something... fitting about our partnership."

Blackwood's thoughts turned to the challenges ahead as they walked. The Order of the Eternal Flame was a formidable adversary, shrouded in secrecy and wielding unknown power. Yet here they were, a determined journalist and a haunted detective, daring to challenge forces beyond their comprehension.

"We're treading a dangerous path," Blackwood mused aloud, his words half-lost in the fog. "But I can't help but feel that together, we stand a chance of bringing light to this darkness."

Blackwood's piercing blue eyes scanned the misty street, his senses heightened by the eerie quiet. He found himself acutely aware of

Evelyn's presence beside him, her determination a palpable force that seemed to cut through the fog.

"Your insights are... invaluable, Miss Bradshaw," he admitted, his voice low and measured. "I've long walked these shadowy paths alone, but I'm beginning to see the wisdom in shared burdens."

Evelyn glanced at him, a wry smile playing on her lips. "Are you admitting that even the great Detective Blackwood needs help occasionally?"

"Perhaps," he replied, a hint of amusement coloring his tone. "Though I'd prefer to think of it as a strategic alliance."

As they turned a corner, the looming silhouette of St. Paul's Cathedral emerged from the mist, its dome a ghostly sentinel over the sleeping city. Blackwood's thoughts drifted to the challenges ahead, the web of secrets and occult machinations they sought to unravel.

"The Order's roots run deep," he mused, half to himself. "We'll need every advantage we can muster."

"Then it's fortunate you have a journalist's tenacity at your disposal," Evelyn responded, her voice tinged with fierce determination.

Blackwood nodded, a newfound respect settling in his chest. With her sharp wit and fearless curiosity, this woman might be the key to unlocking the mysteries that had long eluded him. Together, they stood a chance against the darkness that threatened to engulf London.

As they walked on, Blackwood's resolve strengthened. The path ahead was treacherous, but at this moment, shrouded in London's spectral fog, he felt a glimmer of hope. Whatever trials lay ahead, they would face them not as Detectives and journalists but as allies united in purpose.

Chapter 8: Backstory

Detective Arthur Blackwood paused at the threshold of the Arcane Archives, his fingers tracing the worn brass doorknob. The library's windows glowed with a sickly amber light, barely piercing the heavy fog that cloaked the streets of London. He drew a steadying breath, steeling himself for what lay ahead.

As he entered, the musty scent of ancient tomes assailed his nostrils. Rows of towering bookshelves loomed on either side, their contents hidden in shadow. Blackwood's footsteps echoed softly on the creaking floorboards as he walked deeper into the library's depths.

"This place reeks of secrets," he mused, eyes scanning the dimly lit chamber. "How many forbidden mysteries slumber on these shelves?"

A muffled cough drew his attention to a secluded alcove. There, hunched over a rickety table, sat a man whose nervous energy was palpable even from a distance. Blackwood approached cautiously, his hand instinctively moving to rest on the revolver concealed beneath his coat.

"Mr. Blackwood, I presume?" the man whispered, his voice trembling.

"Indeed," Blackwood replied, studying the informant's pallid features. "And you are?"

"It's best if you don't know my name," the man said, glancing furtively over his shoulder. "I was once part of the Order, but now..." He trailed off, his eyes darting to the shadows as if expecting some unseen horror to emerge.

Blackwood leaned in, his voice low and measured. "You have information about Reginald Thornhill?"

The informant nodded, shaking his hands as he retrieved a sealed envelope from his coat.

Everything I know about his past, his education... it's all in here." He thrust the envelope towards Blackwood. "Take it quickly. I shouldn't linger."

A floorboard creaked in the distance as Blackwood's fingers closed around the envelope. The informant jumped, nearly knocking over his chair. "I must go," he hissed, already backing away. "Be careful, Detective. Thornhill's ambition knows no bounds."

Blackwood watched the man scurry away, disappearing into the labyrinth of bookshelves.

He turned the envelope over in his hands, feeling the weight of its contents.

"What secrets do you hold?" he murmured, tracing the seal with his thumb. "And at what cost were you obtained?"

With a final glance at the now-empty alcove, Blackwood tucked the envelope into his coat and returned through the library. The fog seemed to have thickened outside, swallowing the gaslit streets in its ghostly embrace. As he stepped into the night, Blackwood couldn't shake the feeling that he was being watched, unseen eyes boring into him from the impenetrable mist.

Blackwood's fingers trembled slightly as he broke the seal of the envelope, the crackling of paper echoing in the silent library. His piercing blue eyes scanned the faded script as he unfolded the documents, and the world around him seemed to fade away.

The library dissolved, replaced by a grand Victorian manor house. A young boy, no more than seven, sat cross-legged on an ornate rug, surrounded by ancient tomes and flickering candles. Reginald Thornhill's dark eyes gleamed with an unnatural intensity as his father's voice boomed through the study.

"Remember, my son," the elder Thornhill intoned, "you are destined for greatness within the Order. Our bloodline carries the weight of centuries of arcane knowledge."

The scene shifted, and Reginald, now a teenager, stood before a robed assembly. His mother's hand rested on his shoulder, her voice a whisper of pride and ambition. "The Thornhills have always led the Order of the Eternal Flame.

You, Reginald, will surpass us all."

Blackwood blinked, the visions fading as he returned to the present. He looked up at the informant, his voice hoarse. "These documents... they paint a vivid picture of Thornhill's upbringing. But what of his current activities?"

The informant shifted uncomfortably, his eyes darting to the shadows. "I... I shouldn't say more. It's dangerous."

"Please," Blackwood pressed, leaning forward. "Any information could be crucial."

After a long pause, the informant spoke, his voice barely above a whisper. "Thornhill has been attending gatherings. Secret meetings in abandoned churches and forgotten crypts."

Blackwood's mind raced, connecting threads of information. "What kind of gatherings?"

"Dark rituals," the informant breathed, fear evident in his eyes. "Things that should not be spoken of in the light of day."

Blackwood felt a chill run down his spine as the words hung in the air. He thought to himself, "What depths of depravity has Thornhill sunk to in his quest for power? And how far will he go to achieve his perceived destiny?"

"Thank you," Blackwood said aloud, his voice steady despite the turmoil in his mind. "Your information may prove invaluable."

The informant nodded nervously, already backing away. "Be careful, Detective. Thornhill's influence runs deep. Deeper than you can imagine."

As the man disappeared into the shadows, Blackwood sat alone, surrounded by the weight of centuries-old books and the even heavier burden of this new knowledge. The path ahead was shrouded in darkness, but he knew he had to forge ahead, no matter the cost.

Detective Blackwood's piercing blue eyes narrowed as he leaned closer to the trembling informant. "Tell me about the most recent ritual," he urged, his voice low and insistent. "What did Thornhill do?"

The informant's gaze darted nervously around the dimly lit library before he spoke, his words barely audible. "It was... horrifying. Thornhill, he... he manipulated the others. Used them like pawns."

"How so?" Blackwood pressed, his fingers tightening imperceptibly on the arm of his chair.

"He... he convinced three senior members to participate in a blood ritual," the informant stammered, his face ashen. "Promised them power, influence. But it was all a ruse. He drained their life force and used it to unlock a hidden chamber. That's where the ancient book was kept."

Blackwood's mind reeled at the implications. He could almost see Thornhill's cold, calculating eyes as he sacrificed his fellow Order members.

"And the book?" he asked, dreading the answer.

"He has it now," the informant whispered. "God help us all."

Blackwood remained motionless, lost in thought, as the informant hurried away, melting into the fog-shrouded streets of London—the weight of this new information pressed down upon him like a physical force.

"Thornhill's influence within the Order is far greater than I imagined," he mused, a cold dread settling in his stomach. "If he's willing to sacrifice his brethren, what wouldn't he do to achieve his goals?"

The Detective's mind raced, conjuring images of arcane rituals and dark powers unleashed upon an unsuspecting world. He could almost hear the whispers of the ancient book, its forbidden knowledge calling out to those who would seek to wield it.

"The consequences if he succeeds..."

Blackwood shuddered involuntarily. "It would be catastrophic. Not just for London, but for all of humanity."

Rising from his chair, Blackwood moved to the window, gazing out at the gas lamps flickering weakly in the thick fog. The city seemed oblivious to the danger lurking in its shadows, going about its nightly routines, unaware of the malevolent forces at work.

"I must stop him," Blackwood muttered to himself, his resolve hardening. "Whatever the cost."

The carriage lurched to a halt, its wheels sinking into the mud of the overgrown driveway.

Detective Arthur Blackwood stepped out, his boots squelching in the sodden earth, and gazed up at the looming silhouette of Thornhill Manor. The once-grand estate now stood in eerie silence, its windows dark and lifeless, like the hollow eyes of a corpse.

Blackwood approached the front door, his hand instinctively reaching for the revolver concealed beneath his coat. The rusted hinges groaned in protest as he pushed the door open, revealing a cavernous foyer choked with dust and cobwebs.

"Good God," he muttered, his voice barely above a whisper. "What secrets do you hold, Thornhill?"

As he moved deeper into the house, floorboards creaked beneath his feet, each step sending motes of dust swirling in the dim light filtering through grimy windows.

Blackwood's piercing blue eyes darted from corner to corner, ever vigilant for any sign of danger or clue to Reginald's machinations.

In the grand parlor, faded portraits of the Thornhill family seemed to watch his every move. Blackwood paused before a painting of a young Reginald, noting the cold ambition already evident in the boy's eyes.

"Even then," Blackwood thought, 'the seeds of darkness were taking root."

He pressed on, ascending a grand staircase that led to the upper floors. Each room he explored told a tale of faded opulence and lingering malevolence. In what must have once been a child's nursery, Blackwood discovered occult symbols etched into the floorboards, barely visible beneath years of grime.

At last, he came upon the study. This room bore signs of recent use, unlike the rest of the house.

A half-burned candle sat on the massive oak desk, its wax still soft.

"So, you do return here, Thornhill," Blackwood murmured, running his fingers along the desk's surface. "But where have you hidden your secrets?"

His keen eyes caught a slight irregularity in the wood paneling behind the desk, as if in answer.

Blackwood pressed gently, and a soft click opened a hidden compartment.

Inside lay a stack of leather-bound journals, their pages yellowed with age. With trembling hands, Blackwood opened the topmost volume and began to read.

"My God," he breathed, his eyes widening as he absorbed the contents. "Thornhill, what have you done?"

As Blackwood absorbed the shocking contents of Reginald's journals, a soft knock at the study door startled him from his reverie. He swiftly tucked the journals into his coat and faced the unexpected visitor.

"Detective Blackwood, I presume?" A wizened man with spectacles perched on his nose stepped into the room. "I'm Dr. Everett Holbrook, formerly Professor Winthrop's research assistant. I hoped I might find you here."

Blackwood's eyes narrowed. "And how did you know to look for me, Dr. Holbrook?"

The old historian chuckled softly. "When one has spent decades studying the arcane, one develops a certain... intuition about these matters. May we speak candidly about Reginald Thornhill?"

Blackwood hesitated, then nodded. "What can you tell me about him?"

"Reginald was always... ambitious," Holbrook began, his voice tinged with admiration and fear. "Even as a young scholar, his appetite for forbidden knowledge was insatiable. He would stop at nothing to uncover the darkest secrets of the Order."

"And Winthrop? What was his involvement?"

Holbrook's face darkened. "Algernon tried to guide him, to temper that ambition with wisdom. But Reginald... he saw morality as a weakness, a chain holding him back from true power."

As they spoke, Blackwood's mind raced, piecing together the fragments of information.

"The ancient book," he murmured. "That's what he's after, isn't it?"

"Indeed," Holbrook confirmed, his voice barely above a whisper. "And heaven help us all if he obtains it. The rituals described within could tear the very fabric of reality asunder."

Blackwood felt a chill run down his spine. "Thank you, Dr. Holbrook. Your insights have been invaluable."

As the historian took his leave, Blackwood gathered his thoughts. The weight of the journals in his coat seemed to grow heavier with each passing moment. He knew he had to act quickly before Thornhill's plans could come to fruition.

Descending the manor's grand staircase, Blackwood's footsteps echoed in the empty halls. The fog outside had thickened, transforming the grounds into a spectral landscape. A voice like gravel scraped the silence as he reached for the door handle.

"I wouldn't do that if I were you, Detective."

Blackwood whirled around, his hand instinctively reaching for his revolver. A figure stood in the shadows, face obscured by the brim of a wide hat.

"Who are you?" Blackwood demanded, his voice steady despite the hammering of his heart.

The figure took a step forward, still shrouded in darkness. "Consider me a... concerned party. Your investigation has stirred up dangerous forces, Detective. Forces beyond your comprehension."

Blackwood's jaw clenched. "Is that a threat?"

A low chuckle emanated from the shadows. "A warning, nothing more. Cease your meddling now while you still can. Some secrets are better left buried."

"And if I refuse?" Blackwood challenged, his grip tightening on his weapon.

The figure retreated back into the darkness.

"Then may God have mercy on your soul, for Thornhill certainly won't."

As quickly as it had appeared, the shadowy presence vanished, leaving Blackwood alone in the foyer. The Detective's mind raced, weighing the dangers ahead against the consequences of inaction. With a grim determination, he pushed open the manor's heavy doors and stepped out into the fog-shrouded night.

"Whatever the cost," he thought, "I must see this through to the end."

The fog clung to Detective Arthur Blackwood like a damp shroud as he trudged through the labyrinthine streets of London. Gas lamps flickered weakly, their light barely penetrating the murk. His footsteps echoed off cobblestones slick with mist as he made his way to his office, his mind a maelstrom of dark possibilities.

Upon entering his sanctuary, Blackwood shrugged off his sodden coat and slumped into the worn leather chair behind his desk. The shadows in the corners seemed to dance in the flickering candlelight, mirroring the tumultuous thoughts swirling in his mind.

"Reginald Thornhill," he muttered, steepling his fingers beneath his chin. "What manner of man are you truly?"

He reached for the documents procured earlier, spreading them across his desk like a macabre tarot reading. His piercing blue eyes scanned the pages, connecting threads of information into a tapestry of conspiracy.

"The Order of the Eternal Flame," Blackwood mused aloud, barely above a whisper. "A brotherhood steeped in arcane knowledge, now twisted by Thornhill's ambitions."

He rose, pacing the confines of his office. "But to what end? Power, certainly, but power over what?"

The Detective's gaze fell upon a faded map of London pinned to the wall. He traced the city's veins with a finger, pondering the reach of Thornhill's influence.

"If he succeeds in harnessing the book's power," Blackwood said, his voice tight with concern, "it won't just be the Order at risk. The very fabric of our world could unravel."

He turned back to his desk, resolved to harden his features. "I cannot allow that to happen. No matter the cost."

Blackwood pulled out a fresh sheet of paper, dipping his pen in ink. "To truly understand Thornhill's plans, I must dig deeper into his past.

Every monster has its origin, and I intend to unearth his."

As he began to outline his next steps, a grim smile played at the corners of his mouth. "You may have your secrets, Reginald Thornhill, but I have faced darkness. And I will not rest until I've dragged yours into the light."

The candle guttered, casting long shadows across the room. Outside, the fog thickened as if nature sought to obscure the truth. But Detective Blackwood worked tirelessly within his office, his determination a beacon against the encroaching night.

Chapter 9: Rising Tension

The gas lamps flickered feebly through the dense fog as Detective Arthur Blackwood and Evelyn Bradshaw made their way deeper into the labyrinthine alleys of London's underworld.

Their footsteps echoed ominously off the damp cobblestones, each sound amplified in the eerie silence.

Blackwood's senses were on high alert, his eyes scanning the murky shadows for any sign of movement. He could feel Evelyn's presence beside him, her vigilance a palpable force.

"We're getting close," Blackwood murmured, his voice low. "I can feel it."

Evelyn nodded, her eyes narrowed as she peered into the gloom. "The air feels... different here. Heavier somehow."

Blackwood knew precisely what she meant.

The atmosphere was thicker than the fog, and an oppressive weight seemed to press down on them from all sides. He'd felt it before, in places where the veil between worlds grew thin.

They rounded a corner, the alley narrowing further. Blackwood's hand instinctively moved to the revolver at his hip.

"Stay close," he warned Evelyn. "We don't know what—"

A sudden, bone-chilling breeze swept through the alley, cutting off his words. It howled past them with unnatural force, causing both to stumble. Blackwood's coat whipped around him as he steadied himself against a grimy brick wall.

The wind died away as quickly as it had come, leaving an unsettling stillness. Blackwood turned to Evelyn, their eyes meeting in silent communication. He saw his certainty reflected in her gaze—this was no ordinary gust of wind.

"Arthur," Evelyn breathed, her usual confidence tinged with a hint of trepidation. "What was that?"

Blackwood's jaw tightened as he scanned their surroundings once more. "A warning, perhaps. Or an invitation. Either way, we're not alone here."

He felt the familiar tingling at the back of his neck, the sensation that had guided him through countless encounters with the supernatural. Whatever presence had made itself known, it was close. And it was watching.

The fog thickened with alarming speed, tendrils of mist coiling around their ankles and obscuring the path ahead. Blackwood squinted, straining to discern shapes in the murky gloom. The oppressive atmosphere pressed against his chest, making each breath laborious.

"We're losing visibility fast," Evelyn remarked, her voice tinged with determination. "Arthur, I think we should split up. We'll cover more ground that way."

Blackwood's brow furrowed, his instincts screaming against the idea. "I'm not sure that's wise, Evelyn. There are unseen threats here, lurking in this infernal mist."

Evelyn's eyes flashed with resolve. "Precisely why we need to act quickly. Time isn't on our side, and you know it."

He hesitated, weighing the risks. The fog seemed to writhe around them, alive with evil intent. "It's dangerous," he muttered, more to himself than to her.

"Danger is my stock in trade, detective," Evelyn countered, a hint of her usual bravado returning. "Besides, we both know I can handle myself."

Blackwood sighed, recognizing the stubborn set of her jaw. "Very well," he conceded reluctantly. "But be on your guard. At the first sign of trouble—"

"I'll sing out like a champion whistler," Evelyn finished with a wry smile. "Don't worry so, Arthur. We'll reconvene shortly with a wealth of information to show for it."

He watched as she turned, her silhouette quickly swallowed by the encroaching fog. A knot of worry tightened in his stomach. "Be safe," he whispered into the mist, knowing she could no longer hear him.

Steeling himself, Blackwood pressed forward into the unknown. The Order of the Eternal Flame had left its mark on this forsaken place; he could feel it in his bones. He was determined to uncover clues hidden in the fog, no matter the cost.

The dilapidated warehouse loomed before Blackwood, its weathered facade a stark silhouette against the mist-shrouded night. He approached with measured steps, and his senses heightened to every creak and groan of the ancient structure. As he eased open a rusted door, the hinges protested with an eerie screech that set his teeth on edge.

"Steady now," he murmured to himself, slipping inside. The air within was thick with dust and decay, each breath a struggle against the oppressive atmosphere. Blackwood's eyes, accustomed to piercing shadows, swept the cavernous interior.

His hand instinctively sought the comforting weight of his revolver. "What secrets do you hold?" he whispered to the darkness.

As he ventured deeper, a floorboard groaned beneath his foot. Blackwood froze, listening intently for any sign of disturbance. Silence answered, yet he couldn't shake the feeling of being watched.

"Come now, Arthur," he scolded himself. "Nerves won't serve you here."

His gaze fell upon the far wall, and he drew in a sharp breath. There, barely visible in the gloom, a series of symbols had been etched into the crumbling plaster. Blackwood approached cautiously, his mind racing.

"Curious," he muttered, tracing the air before one particularly intricate glyph. "These are no mere graffiti. The Order's handiwork, without a doubt."

He withdrew a small notebook from his coat, sketching the symbols with deft strokes. A chill crept up his spine as he worked, unbidden and unwelcome.

"What foul purpose do you serve?" Blackwood asked the silent etchings. "And at what cost to those who invoke you?"

The symbols seemed to writhe in the dim light, their eldritch nature defying easy comprehension. Blackwood's jaw clenched, determination overriding his unease.

"I'll decipher your meaning," he vowed quietly. "Whatever dark secrets you hold, they won't remain hidden for long."

Meanwhile, Evelyn Bradshaw crept through the labyrinthine alleys of London's underworld, her senses heightened and alert. The fog clung to her like a second skin, muffling her footsteps as she navigated the treacherous terrain. Her keen eyes darted from shadow to shadow, searching for any sign of movement.

A flicker of candlelight caught her attention, drawing her towards a secluded courtyard. Evelyn pressed herself against the damp brick wall, straining to hear the hushed voices that drifted through the mist.

"The Order grows impatient," a gravelly voice hissed. "The ritual must be completed before the next full moon."

Evelyn's breath caught in her throat. She inched closer, her heart pounding a fierce rhythm against her ribs.

"And what of the detective?" a second voice inquired, tinged with fear. "He draws too close to our secrets."

"Blackwood is of no consequence," the first voice replied dismissively. "Our powers far exceed his mortal comprehension."

Evelyn's mind raced, committing every word to memory. Her fingers twitched, longing for her notebook, but she dared not risk detection.

"The artifacts?" the second voice pressed.

"Secured. The final piece will be in our possession by nightfall tomorrow."

A chill ran down Evelyn's spine. She peered around the corner, catching glimpses of hooded figures huddled in conversation. Their faces were obscured, but she noted their statures, mannerisms, and anything that might later aid in identification.

"By the eternal flame," Evelyn thought, her journalistic instincts aflame with the weight of her discovery, "what dark machinations have I stumbled upon?"

As the group began to disperse, Evelyn pressed further into the shadows. Her heart thundered in her ears, threatening to betray her presence.

When the last echoing footstep faded into the fog, she allowed herself a shaky breath.

"Arthur must know of this immediately," she whispered, barely audible. "But how deep does this conspiracy run? And at what cost will we uncover the truth?"

With one last glance at the now-empty courtyard, Evelyn slipped back into the fog-shrouded streets, her mind awhirl with the gravity of the information she now carried.

A whisper, soft as a dying breath, slithered through the dank air of the dilapidated warehouse. Detective Arthur Blackwood froze, his hand instinctively reaching for the revolver concealed beneath his coat. The silence was deafening, broken only by the faint water drip from rusted pipes overhead.

"Lady Ravenscroft?" Blackwood's voice was barely audible, his blue eyes scanning the gloom.

A pale, shimmering form materialized before him as if summoned by his words. Lady Eleanor Ravenscroft's ethereal beauty was tinged with an unmistakable urgency, her spectral fingers gesturing frantically towards a shadowed corner of the room.

"Arthur," her voice echoed with an otherworldly resonance, "time grows short. The path you seek lies hidden, but I fear what awaits beyond."

Blackwood's brow furrowed, his mind racing.

"What dangers lie ahead, my lady? What secrets does this place hold?"

Lady Ravenscroft's form flickered her expression a mixture of sorrow and determination. "I cannot say with certainty, but the veil between worlds grows thin. Be cautious, Arthur. The Order's influence reaches further than you know."

Following her ethereal guidance, Blackwood approached the wall she indicated. His fingers probed the aged brickwork, searching for any irregularity. "If there's a hidden passage," he muttered, "it's well concealed indeed."

Suddenly, his fingertips caught on a slight protrusion. With a sharp intake of breath, Blackwood applied pressure, and a section of the wall swung inward with a groan of protesting hinges.

"By Jove," he whispered, peering into the impenetrable darkness beyond. "Lady Ravenscroft, I—"

But when he turned, the spectral noblewoman had vanished, leaving him alone with the yawning maw of the secret passage.

Blackwood hesitated, his hand resting on the cold stone of the doorway. "Into the abyss, then," he mused, a wry smile tugging at his lips.

"Let us hope Evelyn's investigations prove as fruitful as mine."

Detective Blackwood stepped into the narrow passage with a deep breath to steel his nerves.

The darkness swallowed him whole as the hidden door creaked shut behind him.

As Blackwood ventured deeper into the passage, the air grew thick and oppressive, each breath a laborious effort. The walls seemed to close in, their damp surface glistening in the feeble light of his lantern. An unidentifiable tension permeated the atmosphere, prickling at his skin and setting his nerves on edge.

"There's something... unnatural about this place," Blackwood murmured, his voice barely above a whisper. He paused, listening intently to the silence that pressed against his eardrums.

"It's as if the very stones are watching, waiting."

A sudden chill swept through the passage, extinguishing his lantern and plunging him into darkness. Blackwood's hand instinctively went to his revolver, his heart pounding.

"Show yourself!" he commanded, his voice steady despite the fear coursing through his veins. "I know you're there, whatever you are."

A low, menacing chuckle echoed from the shadows, seeming to come from everywhere and nowhere. Blackwood's eyes strained in the darkness, desperately seeking any sign of movement.

"What manner of creature are you?" he demanded, backing slowly against the wall. "What is your purpose here?"

The laughter ceased abruptly, replaced by an eerie silence. Blackwood held his breath, every muscle in his body taut with anticipation. Then, a voice - cold and ancient - whispered in his ear:

"We are the guardians of secrets long buried, mortal. Turn back now, lest you share their fate."

Blackwood's mind raced, weighing his options.

"I cannot," he replied firmly, steeling his resolve. "Too much depends on what lies ahead. I must press on, whatever the cost."

Meanwhile, in another part of London's foggy underworld, Evelyn Bradshaw's heart pounded with excitement and trepidation as she approached the group of suspicious figures huddled in conversation. Her journalistic instincts screamed that this was the lead she'd been waiting for.

"Gentlemen," she called out, her voice clear and unwavering. "I couldn't help but overhear your fascinating discussion. Might I trouble you for a moment of your time?"

The group fell silent, their eyes widening in surprise at her sudden appearance. Evelyn noted their reactions, cataloging every twitch and nervous glance.

"Who are you?" one of the men demanded, his hand moving suspiciously towards his coat pocket. "This is no place for a lady."

Evelyn's lips curved into a disarming smile. "Oh, I beg to differ. The most interesting stories often lurk in the most unexpected places. Now, tell me about this 'Order' you were discussing. It sounds positively intriguing."

The fog swirled around Detective Arthur Blackwood as he emerged from the hidden passageway, his senses still reeling from the otherworldly encounter. His eyes scanned the murky alleyway, searching for any sign of Evelyn. A flicker of movement caught his attention, and he saw her familiar silhouette materialize through the mist.

"Evelyn," he called out, his voice low and urgent. "What did you discover?"

She hurried towards him, her face flushed with excitement and trepidation. "Arthur, it's worse than we imagined. The Order... they're planning something catastrophic."

Blackwood's brow furrowed, his piercing blue eyes meeting Evelyn's. "Tell me everything."

As Evelyn recounted her confrontation with the suspicious group, Blackwood's expression grew increasingly grim. His mind raced, connecting the cryptic symbols he'd uncovered with the information Evelyn had extracted.

"Good God," he muttered, gripping his tousled hair. "If you're saying it is true, we have precious little time."

Evelyn nodded, her voice tight with urgency. "We need to act quickly, Arthur. The Order's plans involve some sort of ritual that could tear the fabric of our world apart."

Blackwood's jaw clenched. "Then we must-"

His words were cut short by a sudden, bone-chilling wind that howled through the alley. The gas lamps flickered violently, casting wildly dancing shadows on the brick walls.

"What in heaven's name?" Evelyn gasped, instinctively moving closer to Blackwood.

The Detective's hand moved to his revolver, his eyes darting about. "We're not alone," he growled. "Something's coming."

As if in response to his words, an unearthly shriek pierced the air. The cobblestones beneath their feet began to tremble, and objects—loose bricks, discarded bottles, even small crates—rose into the air, swirling in a chaotic vortex around them.

"Poltergeist activity," Blackwood shouted over the din. "We need to get out of here, now!"

Evelyn's eyes widened in alarm. "Which way?"

Blackwood grabbed her hand, pulling her close. "Stay with me," he ordered. "We'll have to navigate this labyrinth together."

Blackwood's mind raced as they began to move, dodging flying debris and struggling against the supernatural wind. Was this the work of the Order or something even more sinister? Whatever the cause, one thing was clear—their investigation had stirred up forces beyond their comprehension, and escape was now their only option.

With hearts pounding and breath ragged, Blackwood and Evelyn burst through a rusted iron gate, emerging from the oppressive gloom of the underworld into the marginally less menacing fog of London's streets. The Detective stumbled, catching himself against a rain-slicked lamppost. At the same time, Evelyn leaned heavily against a weathered brick wall, her chest heaving.

For a moment, only their labored breathing punctuated the eerie silence of the deserted thoroughfare. Blackwood's piercing blue eyes scanned their surroundings, alert for any signs of pursuit—supernatural or otherwise.

"I believe we've evaded the worst of it," he murmured, his voice low and gravelly.

Evelyn straightened, smoothing her disheveled attire with trembling hands. "That was... unlike anything I've ever experienced," she admitted, a hint of awe coloring her tone.

Blackwood turned to her, his expression grave. "Miss Bradshaw, I'm afraid we've only just begun to see the terrible things that are coming."

Their eyes met, and a wordless understanding passed between them. Evelyn's chin lifted, her jaw set with determination.

"Then we press on," she declared, her voice steady despite the lingering fear in her eyes. "The Order must be stopped, whatever the cost."

Blackwood nodded, a hint of admiration flickering across his features. "Indeed. Though the path ahead is dangerous, we cannot falter now."

As they began to walk, their footsteps echoing off the cobblestones, Blackwood's mind churned with the gravity of their situation. The symbols in the warehouse, the whispers from beyond—all pointed to a conspiracy far more vast and insidious than he had initially believed.

And yet, glancing at Evelyn's resolute figure beside him, he felt a surge of hope.

"We make a formidable team, Miss Bradshaw," he remarked, allowing a rare smile to soften his features.

Evelyn's answering smile was tinged with wry humor. "Indeed, we do, Detective. Though I daresay our adversaries will come to rue the day, they crossed our path."

As they vanished into the swirling fog, their silhouettes merging with the ghostly veil of London's streets, Blackwood and Evelyn steeled themselves for the challenges ahead. The truth awaited, shrouded in darkness and danger—but they would uncover it, come what may.

Chapter 10: Midpoint Reveal

The study door creaked open, admitting a sliver of flickering candlelight that danced across the dust-laden floorboards. Detective Arthur Blackwood stepped inside, his keen eyes sweeping the gloomy chamber as Evelyn Bradshaw followed close behind.

"Good heavens," Evelyn whispered, her gaze roving over towering bookshelves crammed with ancient tomes. "What secrets lie hidden in this sanctum?"

Blackwood's lips tightened as he surveyed the peculiar artifacts adorning the shelves—a shrunken head, an ornate dagger, and crystals that seemed to pulse with an inner light. Each item hinted at dark forces beyond mortal ken.

"We must tread carefully, Miss Bradshaw," he murmured. "Evil lurks in the very air here."

They approached a massive oak desk, its surface obscured by a thick layer of dust save for a curious rectangle where some object had recently rested. Blackwood's brow furrowed as he pondered what item had been removed - and why.

As they drew nearer, a leather-bound volume caught Blackwood's eye. It lay open upon the desk, its yellowed pages covered in odd symbols and diagrams.

"Look here," he said, gesturing for Evelyn to join him. "What do you make of this?"

Evelyn leaned in, her sharp eyes scanning the cryptic text. "How utterly fascinating," she breathed. "I've never seen such peculiar script before."

Blackwood nodded gravely. "Nor have I, in all my years investigating the arcane. This bears further scrutiny."

As they bent over the mysterious tome, the candle's flame guttered in a phantom breeze.

Shadows danced wildly on the walls as if stirred to life by their intrusion. Blackwood felt a chill race down his spine, his every instinct screaming that they had stumbled upon something best left undisturbed.

Yet his resolve remained firm. Whatever this book's dark purpose, he would uncover the truth - no matter the cost.

Evelyn's brow furrowed in concentration as she traced her finger along the intricate symbols.

Suddenly, her eyes widened with realization.

"Arthur, look here," she whispered urgently.

"These markings... they're not random. There's a pattern, a repetition every seventh character."

Blackwood leaned in closer, his piercing blue eyes scanning the page. "By Jove, you're right," he murmured, a mixture of admiration and trepidation in his voice. "It's a cipher and a complex one at that."

As they bent over the book, the old house groaned around them as if protesting their intrusion into long-buried secrets. Blackwood's mind raced, considering the implications of their discovery. What dark knowledge lay hidden within these cryptic pages?

"We must decipher this quickly," Evelyn urged, her voice barely above a whisper. "Who knows what secrets it might reveal about the Order?"

Blackwood nodded grimly. "Indeed. But we must exercise caution. The wrong eyes upon this information could spell disaster."

They worked in hushed tones, their heads close together as they puzzled over the symbols. The occasional creak of floorboards or distant window rattle in the wind made them both start, and their nerves stretched taut as bowstrings.

"I believe I've found the key," Evelyn breathed, her eyes alight with triumph. "Look here, this symbol corresponds to—"

A loud thump from somewhere in the house cut her off mid-sentence. Blackwood's hand instinctively went to his revolver as he scanned the shadowy corners of the study.

"Time grows short," he muttered, returning to the cipher. "We must make haste, Miss Bradshaw. I fear we are not alone in this house of secrets."

Blackwood's keen eyes caught a flicker of movement beneath the desk as the final symbol fell into place. "Wait," he murmured, placing a restraining hand on Evelyn's arm.

"There's something..."

He crouched down, running his fingers along the underside of the ancient wood. A soft click rewarded his efforts, and a panel slid open, revealing a hidden compartment.

"Ingenious," Evelyn breathed, her eyes wide with anticipation. "What secrets does it hold, I wonder?"

Blackwood carefully reached the recess, withdrawing a bundle of papers bound with a faded ribbon. "Correspondence," he said, his voice low and tense. "Between members of the Order, if I'm not mistaken."

As they spread the documents across the desk, Evelyn's nimble fingers sorted through them with practiced efficiency. Suddenly, she inhaled sharply, her hand trembling as she held up a particular letter.

"Arthur," she whispered, using his Christian name, betraying her agitation. "This seal... it belongs to Lord Percival Ashford."

Blackwood leaned in, his brow furrowing as he scanned the contents. "Good God," he muttered, the blood draining from his face. "Ashford is The Shadowmaster."

Evelyn's gasp echoed in the stillness of the study. "But that means..."

"It means we're in far graver danger than we realized," Blackwood finished grimly. His mind raced, recalling his interaction with the charming aristocrat. How blind they'd been!

"We must act quickly," Evelyn said, her voice steadying as she regained her composure. "If Ashford is indeed The Shadowmaster, then the very foundations of our society are at risk."

Blackwood nodded, his jaw set with determination. "Indeed, Miss Bradshaw. But we must tread carefully. One false move, and we may find ourselves entangled in a web from which there is no escape."

Blackwood's piercing blue eyes met Evelyn's, a silent understanding passing between them. His expression hardened, the lines of his face etching deeper as the total weight of their discovery settled upon him. "The Order's reach is far greater than we imagined," he said, his voice low and resolute. "But now we have the means to unravel their schemes."

Evelyn nodded, her quick mind already racing ahead. "We must act swiftly, Arthur. These documents are key to exposing Ashford and dismantling the Order's power structure."

"Agreed," Blackwood replied, his hands moving with practiced efficiency as he gathered the papers. "But we cannot risk losing this evidence. One misstep and all could be lost."

Evelyn's eyes lit up with sudden inspiration.

"What if we were to make copies? Duplicate the most crucial pieces?" She reached for her satchel, withdrawing a small notepad and pencil. "I can sketch the seals and transcribe the most damning passages. Should anything happen to the originals?"

"Brilliant, Miss Bradshaw," Blackwood interjected, a rare smile tugging at the corners of his mouth.

"Your journalistic instincts serve us well once again."

Blackwood found his thoughts drifting to the task's enormity as they worked in tandem. Lord Ashford, the Shadowmaster—a man of wealth and influence, is now revealed as the puppeteer behind a sinister cabal. How deep did the corruption run? And more pressingly, how could they hope to stand against such a formidable foe?

"We're embarking on a perilous path," he murmured, almost to himself.

Evelyn paused in her rapid note-taking, her eyes meeting his with unwavering determination. "Perhaps," she acknowledged.

"But it's a path we must tread for the sake of all those who cannot protect themselves from the shadows that threaten to engulf our city."

The air in the study grew thick with tension, each passing moment heightening their sense of urgency. Blackwood's eyes darted between the documents and the shadowy corners of the room, his keen senses alert for any sign of danger. The flickering gaslight cast grotesque shadows on the walls, seeming to writhe and reach toward them with spectral fingers.

"Do you feel it, Miss Bradshaw?" Blackwood whispered, his voice barely audible. "The very air seems to resist our efforts."

Evelyn's pencil scratched feverishly across her notepad. "Indeed," she breathed, not lifting her gaze from her work. "It's as if the room itself conspires against us."

A floorboard creaked in the hallway beyond, and Blackwood's hand instinctively moved to the revolver concealed beneath his coat. He held his breath, listening intently, but the sound did not repeat.

"We must hasten," he urged, gathering the last of the papers. "Lord Ashford's reach is long, and I fear we've already lingered too long in this viper's nest."

Evelyn nodded, tucking her notes securely into her satchel. "What's our next move, Detective? Surely we can't confront Ashford directly, not without more evidence."

Blackwood's brow furrowed in contemplation.

"No, a direct confrontation would be folly. We must unravel more of this conspiracy before we strike. Perhaps there are other members of the Order we can identify, weaker links in the chain."

As they prepared to leave, Blackwood's mind raced with the implications of their discovery.

The Order of the Eternal Flame, with its tentacles spread throughout London's elite—how many innocents had already fallen victim to its machinations?

"We carry with us the fate of countless souls," he mused grimly. "Ashford's plans must be thwarted, whatever the cost."

As Evelyn turned to leave, her gaze caught on a peculiar array of artifacts lining the study's shelves. She paused, her keen journalist's eye drawn to the eclectic collection.

"Arthur," she whispered, her voice tinged with curiosity. "Look at these. They seem out of place, don't they?"

Blackwood stepped closer, his piercing blue eyes scanning the shelves. Amidst dusty tomes and mundane bric-à-brac sat objects of a decidedly occult nature: a silver chalice etched with arcane symbols, a dagger with a blade as black as night, and a small, intricately carved wooden box that seemed to pulse with an inner light.

"Good eye, Evelyn," he murmured, his voice low and measured. "These aren't mere decorations. They reek of ritualistic purpose."

Evelyn's fingers hovered near the wooden box, not quite touching it. "Do you think these might hold more clues about the Order's activities?"

Blackwood's mind raced, weighing the potential risks against the value of further evidence. "It's possible," he replied, his tone cautious. "The Order clearly values symbolism and mystical artifacts. These could be integral to their ceremonies, perhaps even their power."

"Should we take them?" Evelyn asked, her eyes gleaming with the thrill of uncovering another layer of the mystery.

Blackwood shook his head slightly. "Too risky. Ashford would notice their absence immediately. But..." He pulled out a small notebook, quickly sketching the artifacts and jotting down descriptions. "We can research their significance later. Every detail may prove crucial in understanding our enemy."

As they stepped into the hallway, the weight of their discoveries settled upon them like a heavy cloak. The air seemed thicker, charged with an almost palpable tension. Evelyn's usually confident stride faltered slightly.

"Arthur," she whispered, her voice barely audible, "we're in grave danger now, aren't we? Ashford won't stop until he silences us."

Blackwood turned to her, his gaze steady and resolute. "We are," he admitted, his voice low but unwavering. "But remember, Evelyn, we now hold the advantage of knowledge. Ashford doesn't yet know his secret has been compromised."

He placed a reassuring hand on her shoulder.

"We will bring The Shadowmaster to justice, I swear it. Our cause is righteous, and we have truth on our side."

Evelyn's posture straightened, her determination visibly rekindled by Blackwood's words. "You're right," she said, a hint of steel returning to her voice. "We've faced dangers before and face this head-on."

Blackwood's mind churned with plans and contingencies as they moved through the darkened corridor. The path ahead was treacherous, but he felt a grim satisfaction. They had struck the first blow against the Order's veil of secrecy, and he would not rest until Ashford's sinister plans were thwarted.

Their footsteps echoed softly against the worn floorboards as they walked through the dimly lit corridor. The gaslights flickered, casting long, dancing shadows on the faded wallpaper.

Blackwood's keen senses were alert, his eyes darting to every corner and crevice.

"We must tread carefully from here on out," Blackwood murmured, his voice barely above a whisper. "Ashford's influence likely extends far beyond what we've uncovered."

Evelyn nodded, her face a mask of determination. "Do you think he has spies within Scotland Yard?" she asked, matching his hushed tone.

Blackwood's brow furrowed. "It's a possibility we can't discount. The Order's tendrils seem to reach every shadowy corner of London."

As they approached a junction in the hallway, Blackwood paused, his hand instinctively moving to the revolver concealed beneath his coat. The creaking of the old house took on a more sinister quality, as if the very walls were conspiring against them.

"Arthur," Evelyn whispered urgently, "what's our next move?"

Blackwood's mind raced, weighing their options. "We need allies," he replied, his blue eyes gleaming with resolve in the dim light.

"Trustworthy ones. And we must find a secure location to examine these documents more thoroughly."

As they continued their cautious progress, Blackwood couldn't shake the feeling that they were walking a knife's edge. The revelation about Ashford had indeed set them on a perilous path, but with each step, his determination grew stronger. They were no longer fumbling in the dark; they had glimpsed the face of their enemy, and that knowledge would be their guiding light.

Chapter 11: Crisis Point

The hansom cab rattled to a halt, its wheels grinding against the slick cobblestones. Detective Arthur Blackwood emerged, his tall frame silhouetted against the swirling fog that cloaked the streets of London. He pulled his coat tighter, the chill seeping into his bones as surely as the doubts that plagued his mind.

"Much obliged," Blackwood muttered to the cabbie, his piercing blue eyes scanning the murky darkness. The gas lamps flickered feebly, their meager light barely penetrating the gloom.

As he set off toward the police station, each footfall echoed hollowly. The fog muffled the city's usual bustle, leaving an eerie silence in its wake. Blackwood's thoughts raced, a tangle of clues and suspicions that refused to align.

"The Order of the Eternal Flame," he mused aloud, his breath visible in the frigid air. "What infernal game are they playing?"

The police station's looming facade materialized from the mist, its windows glowing with a wan light. Blackwood's pace slowed, his apprehension growing with each step.

"Worthington won't take kindly to my methods," he thought, his jaw tightening. "But damn it all, there's more at play here than he realizes."

The memory of Lady Ravenscroft's ethereal form flashed in his mind, her desperate plea still ringing in his ears. He clenched his fists, steeling himself for the confrontation ahead.

"I cannot falter now," Blackwood whispered, his voice barely audible above the soft patter of drizzle on stone. "Too much hangs in the balance."

As he approached the station's entrance, the weight of isolation pressed upon him. Standing alone in the fog-choked night, Blackwood felt keenly the burden of his unique perspective—a man caught between worlds, seeking justice in realms both seen and unseen.

"Very well, Worthington," he said, squaring his shoulders. "Let us see what your vaunted logic makes of this tangled web."

Detective Blackwood ascended the steps with a deep breath, the mist swirling about his feet as if reluctantly releasing him to his fate.

The heavy oak door creaked open, revealing the dimly lit interior of the police station. Detective Blackwood paused at the threshold, his keen eyes scanning the room until they fell upon the imposing figure of Inspector Worthington. The Inspector stood like a sentinel, his stern visage a mask of disapproval illuminated by flickering gaslight.

Blackwood's hand tightened imperceptibly on the doorframe as he gathered his resolve.

"Steady now," he thought, his mind racing. "Every word must count."

With measured steps, he entered the station, the floorboards groaning beneath his feet. The air was thick with tension, punctuated only by the soft ticking of a wall clock.

"Blackwood," Worthington's gruff voice cut through the silence. "I trust you have a good explanation for your... unorthodox methods."

Blackwood met the Inspector's gaze, his blue eyes unwavering. "Inspector," he replied, his tone carefully modulated. "I assure you, every action I've taken has been in pursuit of justice."

Worthington's eyes narrowed. "Justice? Or wild speculation? Your reports read like penny dreadfuls, Blackwood. Ghostly apparitions and secret societies? This is a murder investigation, not a séance!"

"With all due respect, Inspector," Blackwood countered, fighting to keep his frustration in check, "there are forces at work here beyond our conventional understanding. The evidence—"

"Evidence?" Worthington scoffed. "You mean your intuitions and fever dreams? We deal in facts, Detective. Cold, hard facts."

Blackwood's mind raced, searching for the right words to bridge the chasm between their perspectives. "Facts can be deceptive, Inspector. What we see is not always the full truth."

Worthington's face hardened, his jaw clenching visibly. "Enough of this nonsense, Blackwood. Let me show you what real evidence looks like."

The Inspector strode to his desk, retrieving a thick folder. He slammed it down, the sound echoing in the cramped office. Blackwood's piercing blue eyes followed Worthington's every move, his frustration simmering beneath the surface.

"Here," Worthington declared, spreading photographs and reports. "Witness statements, forensic analysis, and timeline reconstructions. All were pointing to a straightforward case of revenge killing."

Blackwood leaned in, his keen mind absorbing the details. Each piece of evidence seemed to chip away at his theories, logical explanations replacing the whispers of the supernatural he'd been chasing.

"You see, Detective," Worthington continued, his voice laced with smug satisfaction, "no need for ghostly ladies or secret cults. Just a jilted lover with a motive and opportunity."

Blackwood's brow furrowed, his thoughts racing. "But the symbols at the crime scene," he countered, "the unexplained cold spots, the—"

"Coincidences and superstition," Worthington interrupted. "Nothing more."

As the Inspector continued his methodical dismantling of Blackwood's case, the Detective found himself grappling with doubt. Had his intuition led him astray? Were the horrors he'd witnessed merely tricks of an overactive imagination?

"No," Blackwood thought, steeling himself.

"There's more here, I can feel it. I must find a way to make him understand."

Blackwood drew a deep breath, his piercing blue eyes locking onto Worthington's stern gaze. "Inspector," he began, his voice low and measured, "I implore you to consider the broader implications. The Order of the Eternal Flame is no mere flight of fancy."

Worthington's lips curled into a skeptical sneer.

"Go on then, Detective. Enlighten me."

"The victim's wounds," Blackwood pressed on, leaning forward, "they weren't just random cuts. They formed a pattern, a sigil used by the Order in their unholy rituals. And the missing heart—"

"Sensationalism," Worthington cut in, his tone sharp. "You're grasping at shadows, Blackwood."

The Detective's frustration mounted, a war waging within him. He could feel the truth of his convictions, yet doubt gnawed at the edges of his mind. "The evidence may seem circumstantial," he admitted, "but the urgency of this matter cannot be overstated. If the Order succeeds in their plans—"

"Plans?" Worthington scoffed. "What plans, Blackwood? You've yet to provide a shred of concrete evidence that this... Order even exists."

Blackwood's fists clenched at his sides, his voice on a pleading edge. "I've seen things, Inspector. Horrors that defy explanation. The Order's influence runs deep, corrupting the very fabric of our society."

As he spoke, Blackwood's mind raced. Had he truly uncovered a vast conspiracy, or was he chasing phantoms? The weight of his experiences pressed against the cold logic of Worthington's arguments, leaving him adrift in a sea of uncertainty.

"Your intuition, your 'sixth sense,'" Worthington's voice dripped with disdain, "they have no place in a proper investigation. I need facts, Blackwood. Hard evidence. Without it, I'm forced to stop this search for something that doesn't exist."

Blackwood's body tensed, his knuckles turning white as he clenched his fists tighter. A deep furrow etched itself across his brow, casting shadows over his piercing blue eyes. He swallowed hard, fighting to maintain his composure as Worthington's skepticism bore down upon him.

"Inspector," Blackwood began, his voice wavering slightly, "I implore you to reconsider. The stakes are—"

"Enough!" Worthington thundered, slamming his palm on the desk. The sound reverberated through the room, causing Blackwood to flinch involuntarily. "I've indulged your theories long enough, Blackwood. Here's how it stands: you have forty-eight hours to bring me irrefutable evidence. Tangible proof of this Order's existence and their connection to the murder. If you fail to do so, I'll have no choice but to terminate your involvement in this case. Is that clear?"

The ultimatum hung in the air like a guillotine blade, poised to sever Blackwood's investigation. He felt a chill creep down his spine, his breath catching in his throat as he processed the gravity of Worthington's words.

"Two days," Blackwood murmured, his mind racing through potential leads. "It's not much time, but—"

"It's all you're getting," Worthington interrupted, his tone brooking no argument. "Don't make me regret even this small concession, Detective."

As Blackwood stood there, he could almost feel the fog from outside seeping into the room, clouding his thoughts and obscuring the path forward. How could he hope to unravel such an intricate web of deceit in a mere two days?

Blackwood closed his eyes for a moment, drawing a deep breath. The flickering gaslight cast dancing shadows across his furrowed brow as he gathered his thoughts. Lady Ravenscroft's spectral visage swam before his mind's eye, her ethereal voice echoing in his memory: "Only you can uncover the truth, Detective Blackwood. The fate of many rests upon your shoulders."

He opened his eyes, meeting Worthington's stern gaze with renewed resolve. "Inspector," Blackwood began, his voice low and measured, "I understand your skepticism. But I beseech you to consider the broader implications of this case."

Worthington's eyebrow arched. "And what implications might those be, Detective?"

Blackwood leaned forward, his piercing blue eyes alight with urgency. "The Order of the Eternal Flame is not merely a group of eccentric occultists. Their influence reaches far beyond what we initially believed. If my suspicions are correct, they pose a threat not just to individuals but to the very fabric of our society."

He paused, noting a flicker of uncertainty cross Worthington's features. Seizing the moment, Blackwood pressed on. "Think, Inspector. The victims we've encountered and the patterns we've uncovered all point to a conspiracy of unprecedented scale. If we shut this investigation down now, we risk allowing a malevolent force to operate unchecked in the shadows of our city."

Worthington's jaw clenched, his fingers drumming on the desk. "Your words paint a dire picture, Blackwood. But without concrete evidence—"

"Evidence I can gather, given time and resources," Blackwood interjected, his voice tinged with desperation. "I implore you, Inspector. Grant me the latitude to pursue this case to its fullest extent. The consequences of inaction could be catastrophic."

As the words hung in the air, Blackwood could see the conflict raging behind Worthington's eyes. The Inspector's resolute exterior wavered, if only for a moment.

Detective Arthur Blackwood stepped out of the police station, the heavy oak door slamming shut behind him with a finality that echoed his tumultuous thoughts. The fog, which had been a mere nuisance earlier, now seemed to engulf him entirely, a suffocating blanket that mirrored the uncertainty clouding his mind.

He paused at the top of the stone steps, his keen eyes scanning the misty street below. The gas lamps flickered weakly, their light barely penetrating the gloom. A solitary hansom cab clattered past, its driver hunched against the chill, oblivious to the Detective's internal struggle.

"Confound it all," Blackwood muttered, his breath visible in the frigid air. He descended the steps, each footfall echoing in the eerie silence of the night. The cobblestones beneath his feet were slick with moisture, a treacherous path much like the case that now seemed to be slipping from his grasp.

He halted abruptly at the corner, one hand pressed against the cold brick of a nearby building. His mind raced, replaying the confrontation with Worthington. Had he pushed too far? Not far enough? The weight of Lady Ravenscroft's plea bore down upon him, a spectral burden he could not shake.

"I cannot falter now," he whispered to himself, his voice barely audible above the distant rumble of the city. "There's too much at stake."

As if in response to his words, a gust of wind stirred the fog, and for a brief moment, Blackwood could have sworn he saw the ethereal outline of Lady Ravenscroft's form in the swirling mist. Her sorrowful eyes seemed to bore into his very soul, reigniting the spark of determination that had brought him this far.

Blackwood straightened his posture, adjusting his coat with renewed purpose. "Very well, my lady," he said softly to the dissipating apparition.

"I shall not abandon this quest, no matter the obstacles that lie ahead."

With a deep breath, he steeled himself against the chill and the doubt that threatened to consume him. The path forward was shrouded in uncertainty, but Arthur Blackwood was no stranger to navigating the unknown. He took a step into the fog-choked street, his mind already formulating the next move in this intricate game of shadows and secrets.

Blackwood's footsteps echoed softly on the damp cobblestones as he ventured deeper into the murky labyrinth of London's streets. The gas lamps cast feeble halos in the mist, their light barely penetrating the gloom that enveloped him.

"Worthington be damned," he muttered, his breath visible in the chill air. "There's more at work here than his rational mind can fathom."

As he walked, Blackwood's piercing blue eyes darted from shadow to shadow, ever vigilant.

The weight of his revolver pressed reassuringly against his side, a cold comfort in this world of warmth-leaching fog.

His mind raced, piecing together the fragments of the case. "The Order of the Eternal Flame," he mused aloud, his voice low and measured.

"What secrets do you guard behind your veil of mysticism?"

A figure materialized from the mist ahead, causing Blackwood to tense momentarily. But it was merely a constable on his nightly rounds who nodded respectfully as they passed.

"Evening, Detective," the man said, his tone curious. "Bit late for a stroll, ain't it?"

Blackwood managed a thin smile. "The hour grows late, but evil never sleeps, constable. Keep your wits about you tonight."

Blackwood's thoughts turned inward once more as the constable's form faded into the fog behind him. The memory of Lady Ravenscroft's plea echoed in his mind, spurring him onward.

He clenched his fists, feeling the familiar fire of determination ignite within his chest.

"I'll not rest until I've unraveled this mystery," he vowed to the silent streets. "No matter the cost."

With each step, Blackwood's resolve strengthened. The fog seemed to part before him as if recognizing the unyielding spirit that drove him forward into the unknown. Soon, his silhouette began to fade, swallowed by the mist and the night, leaving behind only the echo of his footsteps and the promise of truths yet to be uncovered.

Chapter 12: Dark Night of the Soul

Detective Arthur Blackwood sat motionless in his study, the flickering candlelight casting eerie shadows across his gaunt features. His hands rested atop a stack of case notes, but his piercing blue eyes were unfocused, staring into the murky depths of his own troubled mind.

The silence pressed in around him, broken only by the faint ticking of the mantel clock. Arthur's thoughts churned like the infamous London fog, swirling and obscuring the truth he desperately sought.

"What am I missing?" he muttered, running a hand through his disheveled dark hair. "The clues are there, just beyond my grasp, like phantoms in the mist."

He rose and began to pace, each step measured and deliberate. The floorboards creaked beneath his feet, a discordant melody accompanying the tumult of his inner dialogue.

"Am I truly equipped to confront these otherworldly forces?" Arthur wondered his voice barely a whisper. "Or am I a fool, chasing shadows and apparitions?"

The weight of doubt settled over him like a shroud, as heavy and oppressive as the fog that cloaked the streets outside. He paused by the window, peering out at the gloom. Gas lamps flickered dimly, their light barely penetrating the thick haze.

"This cursed fog," he mused, "mirrors this case's obscurity. Each turn reveals new mysteries, new depths of darkness I scarcely comprehend."

Arthur's hand trembled slightly as he reached for the candle, bringing it closer to illuminate the papers on his desk. His eyes scanned the notes, searching for a thread of logic in the tapestry of the supernatural.

"I've faced the unexplainable before," he reminded himself, his tone gaining a hint of steel. "Each encounter has left its mark, yes, but also honed my intuition."

Yet a chill ran down his spine even as he spoke the words. The shadows seemed to lengthen, reaching out with ethereal fingers. Arthur squared his shoulders, fighting back against the encroaching dread.

"I cannot falter now," he declared, his voice echoing in the stillness of the room. "Too many lives hang in the balance. Too many souls cry out for justice."

He returned to his chair, pulling the papers close. With renewed determination, he began to sift through the evidence again, his keen mind probing for connections others might overlook.

"There must be a pattern," Arthur muttered, "a key to unlock this infernal puzzle. I shall not rest until I find it."

As the candle burned low, Detective Blackwood continued his vigil. He was a solitary figure battling against the encroaching darkness within and without.

Like the caress of silk against stone, a soft whisper slithered through the study. Arthur's head snapped up, his piercing blue eyes darting to the room's corners. The hairs on the nape of his neck stood on end, a primal warning of something beyond mortal ken.

"Who's there?" he demanded, his voice steady despite his pulse quickening. The shadows seemed to writhe in response, merging into a familiar and impossibly alien form.

From the inky darkness emerged a figure of ethereal beauty. Lady Eleanor Ravenscroft materialized with the grace of mist rising from a still lake. Her translucent form shimmered in the candlelight, a gossamer gown flowing around her like liquid starlight.

Arthur's breath caught in his throat. Lady Ravenscroft's presence filled the room with an otherworldly chill, yet her eyes held a warmth that seemed to pierce the veil between life and death.

"Lady Ravenscroft," Arthur whispered, his analytical mind warring with the impossible vision before him. "I... I had not expected..."

The spectral noblewoman's lips curved into a smile tinged with sorrow. "Few ever do, Detective Blackwood. Yet here I stand, a bridge between your world and the next."

Arthur's fingers tightened on the arm of his chair, anchoring him to reality even as it threatened to slip away. "Why have you come?" he asked, his Detective instincts rising. What secrets do you bring from beyond the grave?"

Lady Ravenscroft's form rippled as if stirred by an unseen breeze. "Answers, Arthur," she replied, her voice an echo of centuries past.

"And perhaps, if you are willing, the strength to face what lies ahead."

Arthur rose from his chair with exquisite care, his movements slow and deliberate as if approaching a rare and delicate artifact. His piercing blue eyes never left Lady Ravenscroft's ethereal form, drinking in every shimmering detail. The floorboards creaked softly beneath his feet, each step measured and cautious.

"Strength, my lady?" he inquired, his voice a low, controlled rumble that belied the tumult of emotions roiling within. "I fear my own has been sorely tested of late."

Lady Ravenscroft's spectral form drifted closer, the air around her crackling with an otherworldly energy. When she spoke, her words carried the weight of ages, tinged with an empathy that transcended mortal bounds.

"You possess more than you know, Detective," she intoned in a melody of whispers and echoes. I have watched you, Arthur Blackwood. Your dedication and unwavering pursuit of justice are not mere traits, but the essence of your being."

Arthur's brow furrowed, his analytical mind grappling with the implications of her words.

"You've been observing me? For how long? And to what purpose?"

A sad smile graced Lady Ravenscroft's translucent features. "Time holds little meaning for those beyond the veil. But know this: your quest and mine are intertwined. The darkness that shrouds this city is a shadow I have known all too well."

Arthur felt a curious warmth spreading through his chest as she spoke, dispelling the chill in his bones. It was as if her presence was rekindling a flame of determination, he had long extinguished.

Arthur's fingers curled into fists at his sides, his knuckles whitening as he fought to maintain his composure. "Lady Ravenscroft," he began, his voice barely above a whisper, "the weight of this case... it threatens to crush me. Each night, I'm haunted by the faces of those I couldn't save, by the darkness that seems to grow stronger with each passing hour."

He turned away, unable to meet her ethereal gaze. "I fear... I fear I'm not equal to the task before me. That my failures will doom not just myself but all of London."

Lady Ravenscroft's form shimmered, a ripple of compassion passing through her spectral visage. She glided closer, her presence a soothing balm to Arthur's troubled soul.

"Detective Blackwood," she said, her voice carrying the gentle wisdom of centuries, "it is precisely your capacity to feel such a burden that makes you worthy of bearing it. Your doubts are not weakness but a reflection of your profound understanding of what's at stake."

Arthur's eyes met hers, finding an unexpected strength in their ghostly depths.

"Remember the Whitechapel case," she continued, "how you persevered when all others had given up hope. Or the Blackfriar's Bridge incident, where your intuition saved countless lives. These were not mere happenstance, Arthur. They were a testament to your extraordinary ability to confront the darkness and emerge victorious."

Her words stirred memories within him—moments of triumph snatched from the jaws of despair. Arthur felt a familiar resolve beginning to crystalize in his chest, pushing back against the tide of doubt that had threatened to overwhelm him.

Arthur inhaled deeply, the scent of old parchment and candle wax mingling with the otherworldly fragrance that accompanied Lady Ravenscroft's presence. He straightened his posture, his piercing blue eyes reflecting the flickering candlelight as he considered her words.

"You speak of resilience, my lady," he said, his voice low and measured. "But how does one remain steadfast when faced with forces beyond mortal comprehension?"

Lady Ravenscroft's form seemed to brighten, her ethereal beauty radiating a gentle warmth that pushed back the encroaching shadows.

"By recognizing, Detective, that you possess a power that transcends the ordinary. Your intuition and unwavering pursuit of truth are weapons as potent as any supernatural force."

Arthur's brow furrowed in contemplation. "I've always relied on logic, on evidence. But this case... it defies conventional reasoning."

"Then you must evolve, Arthur," she replied, her spectral hand gesturing towards the papers on his desk. As you've done countless times before, your journey from doubt to determination is not a straight path but a winding road that tests and strengthens you with each turn."

He nodded slowly, feeling a spark of his old confidence reigniting. "Perhaps you're right. Perhaps it's time I embrace the unconventional methods that have served me in the past."

Lady Ravenscroft's smile was both encouraging and enigmatic. "Precisely. Your resilience is your ability to adapt and find strength in vulnerability."

A profound silence fell over the study, broken only by the soft crackle of the candle's flame.

Arthur stood motionless, absorbing the weight of Lady Ravenscroft's words. The oppressive atmosphere that had earlier clouded his thoughts began to dissipate, replaced by a newfound clarity.

As he gazed at the ghostly figure before him, Arthur realized that her presence was more than just a supernatural visitation. She was a symbol of hope, a reminder that light was to be found even in the darkest corners of London's fog-shrouded streets.

The shadows in the room seemed to recede, no longer threatening but merely a natural counterpoint to the illumination of understanding that now filled him. Once a tumultuous sea of doubt, Arthur's mind now stilled into a calm pool of resolve.

Arthur Blackwood's hand closed around the papers on his desk, his grip firm and purposeful.

The rustling of parchment cut through the silence as he gathered the documents, each one a piece of the puzzle he was now determined to solve.

"I shall not falter again, Lady Ravenscroft," he declared, his voice low but resonant with newfound conviction. "Your counsel has illuminated the path I must tread, no matter how treacherous it may be."

He turned to face her fully, his piercing blue eyes alight with a fire that had long been dormant. "The darkness that plagues our fair city shall find me a formidable adversary. I swear it."

Lady Ravenscroft's ethereal form shimmered, her outline beginning to blur at the edges. "Your resolve heartens me, Detective," she said, her voice carrying the faintest echo of another realm. "But remember, in your quest for justice, you need not walk alone."

Arthur felt a pang in his chest as he realized their time was drawing to a close. "How can I reach you again?" he asked, a note of urgency creeping into his voice.

"I am bound to this world by the very mystery you seek to unravel," she replied, her form growing more translucent with each passing moment. "Our paths will cross again when the need is greatest."

As Lady Ravenscroft's presence began to fade, Arthur stepped forward, his hand outstretched as if to grasp something intangible. "I shall not disappoint you," he vowed, his words carrying the weight of a solemn oath.

Her smile, radiant and bittersweet, lingered even as her form dissipated. "It is not I you must satisfy, Arthur Blackwood, but the call of justice that echoes in your heart."

With those final words, Lady Ravenscroft vanished, leaving Arthur alone in the study. Yet, he felt anything but solitary. The bond forged between them, transcending the barriers of life and death, filled him with a sense of purpose that went beyond mere duty.

He clutched the papers to his chest, his mind racing with plans and strategies. "The game is afoot," he murmured to himself, echoing the words of a fictional detective he admired. "And this time, I shall see it through to its conclusion, come what may."

Arthur stood alone in the study, his tall figure casting a long shadow across the room. The candle's flame burned steadily, its unwavering light mirroring his newfound resolve. He took a deep breath, filling his lungs with the musty air of his book-lined sanctuary.

"Well then," he muttered to himself, "there's no time like the present to begin."

With deliberate movements, he gathered the scattered papers on his desk and arranged them into a neat pile. His piercing blue eyes scanned the top document, a police report detailing the latest in a string of inexplicable disappearances.

"What connects you all?" Arthur mused aloud, his brow furrowing. "What thread binds these seemingly disparate cases?"

He paced the room's length, his footsteps muffled by the thick carpet. The weight of responsibility settled upon his shoulders, but rather than burdening him, it seemed to invigorate his spirit.

"Lady Ravenscroft believes in me," he thought, a flicker of warmth kindling in his chest. It may be time I started believing in myself as well.

Arthur paused by the window, gazing out at the fog-shrouded streets of London. The gas lamps struggled to penetrate the gloom, their light creating eerie halos in the mist.

"I've faced the unknown before," he reassured himself. "This case may be shrouded in darkness, but I carry the light of truth."

A sudden chill swept through the room as he returned to his desk. The candle flame wavered, casting dancing shadows on the walls. For a moment, Arthur could have sworn he heard a faint whisper, like the echo of Lady Ravenscroft's voice.

"Remember, Arthur," it seemed to say, "you are never truly alone."

A smile tugged at the corners of his mouth.

"Indeed, I am not," he replied to the empty room, feeling a renewed connection to the unseen world that now guided his path. "And with that knowledge, I shall face whatever trials await."

Chapter 13: Plot Twist

The gaslights flickered dimly through the swirling fog as Detective Arthur Blackwood and Evelyn Bradshaw walked briskly down the cobblestone street, their voices low but urgent.

"The Order's influence runs deeper than we imagined," Arthur said, his brow furrowed. "Their tendrils reach into the very heart of Parliament itself."

Evelyn nodded, her eyes gleaming with determination. "Indeed. My sources confirm a clandestine meeting between Lord Ashworth and the Grand Master last week. We're close to unraveling this conspiracy, Arthur."

The detective felt cautious optimism. Their investigation was progressing, and pieces of the puzzle were falling into place. Yet the gravity of what they faced weighed heavily on him.

"We must tread carefully, Evelyn," he warned. "The Order will stop at nothing to protect their secrets."

"I'm well aware of the risks," she replied sharply. "But we cannot falter now, not when we're so close to exposing them."

Arthur couldn't help but admire her courage, even as concern gnawed at him. "Your tenacity is admirable, my dear. But I fear—"

He broke off suddenly, every nerve in his body tensing. The fog seemed to thicken around them, muffling all sound. An unnatural silence descended, broken only by their quiet footsteps.

"Arthur?" Evelyn whispered, her hand instinctively reaching for his arm. "What is it?"

The detective's piercing blue eyes scanned their surroundings, seeking any hint of movement in the murky gloom. A chill that had nothing to do with the damp night air ran down his spine.

"Something's not right," he murmured, his voice barely audible. "We're being watched."

Evelyn's grip on his arm tightened. "The Order?"

Arthur didn't respond, his mind racing. The silence pressed in on them, oppressive and foreboding. Every shadow seemed to hide a potential threat, every alleyway a possible ambush point.

He fought to maintain his composure, years of facing the supernatural steeling his nerves. But a creeping dread whispered that they may have delved too deep into forces beyond their control this time.

"We need to move," he said softly, guiding Evelyn forward with a gentle but insistent pressure. "Quickly and quietly. Don't look back."

As they hurried through the fog-laden streets, Arthur's hand instinctively moved towards the pistol concealed beneath his coat. Whatever danger lurked in the shadows, he was determined to protect Evelyn at all costs.

The fog parted like a spectral curtain, revealing dark figures emerging from the shadows. Before Arthur could react, a tall, imposing man stepped forward—Reginald Thornhill, his eyes gleaming with malice.

"Miss Bradshaw," Thornhill's smooth voice cut through the silence, "I believe you have something that belongs to us."

In an instant, chaos erupted. Two burly men lunged for Evelyn, their hands grasping at her arms. She fought back fiercely, her voice ringing out in the night.

"Arthur! Help!"

Blackwood's instincts kicked in immediately. He threw himself at the nearest assailant, his fist connecting with a satisfying crunch. "Unhand her, you brutes!" he roared, his heart pounding with a mixture of fury and fear.

As he grappled with one attacker, Arthur's mind raced. How had Thornhill found them? What did they want with Evelyn? He had to protect her and stop this madness before it was too late.

"Run, Evelyn!" he shouted, ducking a wild swing from his opponent. "Get to safety!"

But even as the words left his mouth, Arthur saw with horror that Thornhill had seized Evelyn. She struggled valiantly, her eyes wide with determination and fear.

"I won't let you win, Thornhill!" she spat, kicking out at her captor.

Arthur fought with renewed vigor, desperation lending strength to his blows. He had to reach her and save her from whatever nefarious plans Thornhill had in store.

"Let her go!" he demanded, his voice hoarse with exertion. "Your quarrel is with me, Thornhill!"

But for every man he felled, two more seemed to take their place. The fog swirled around them, obscuring his vision and confusing his senses. Arthur's heart sank as he realized he was fighting a losing battle.

"Arthur!" Evelyn's voice rang out again, tinged with despair as Thornhill dragged her towards a waiting carriage.

Arthur broke free from his attackers with a final burst of strength and lunged towards her. Their fingertips brushed for a fleeting moment before she was wrenched away, disappearing into the misty night.

"Evelyn!" he cried, echoing through the empty streets. But it was too late. The carriage wheels clattered on the cobblestones, fading into the distance as Arthur stood alone in the fog, his heart heavy with failure and dread.

Arthur Blackwood stood motionless in the fog-laden street, his chest heaving as he fought to regain his composure. The silence that followed Evelyn's abduction was deafening, broken only by the distant tolling of a church bell. He clenched his fists, willing his racing mind to focus.

"Think, Arthur, think," he muttered, his piercing blue eyes scanning the misty surroundings for any clue left behind. "Every second counts."

As he paced the cobblestones, his mind whirled with possibilities. Why Evelyn? Why now? The pieces of the puzzle began to shift and rearrange themselves in his mind.

"Thornhill," he growled, the name leaving a bitter taste in his mouth. "You've shown your hand at last."

He approached a nearby gas lamp, its flickering light barely penetrating the gloom. Arthur's fingers traced the rough brick of the building beside it, his touch hesitant as if expecting to find some hidden message etched into the stone.

"It's not just about the Order," he mused aloud, his voice low and measured. "Thornhill's ambitions run deeper than we ever suspected."

A chill ran down Arthur's spine as the full implication of Evelyn's kidnapping dawned on him. He turned abruptly, his coat swirling around him as he addressed the empty street.

"You're not just a member, are you, Thornhill? You're orchestrating this whole affair." His words hung in the air, heavy with the weight of revelation. "The Order of the Eternal Flame is merely a pawn in your grand design."

Arthur's mind raced, connecting threads that had seemed disparate before. The mysterious artifacts, the ritualistic murders, and the whispers of ancient power pointed to a conspiracy far more intricate and dangerous than he had initially believed.

"But why Evelyn?" he questioned, his brow furrowing. "What role does she play in your machinations?"

As if in response, a gust of wind cut through the fog, carrying the faint scent of smoke and something else—something arcane and foreboding. Arthur's eyes widened as a new, terrifying possibility took shape in his mind.

"No," he breathed, his voice barely above a whisper. "It can't be. Evelyn, what have you unknowingly stumbled upon?"

With renewed urgency, Arthur strode purposefully down the street, his mind set on unraveling the dark tapestry that Thornhill had woven. The game had changed, and the stakes were higher than ever before.

Arthur clenched his fists, his knuckles whitening beneath his leather gloves. The fog swirled around him, a physical manifestation of the murky danger that threatened to engulf Evelyn.

His jaw set with grim determination as he muttered to himself, "I will find you, Evelyn. Whatever the cost."

He strode forward, each step resonating with purpose. The gas lamps cast elongated shadows that seemed to reach for him, but Arthur pressed on, undeterred. His voice, low and resolute, cut through the eerie silence of the London streets.

"Thornhill may have his conspiracies and his Order, but he underestimates the power of a promise." Arthur's blue eyes flashed with fierce intensity. "And I promise you, Evelyn, I will not rest until you're safe."

As he navigated the labyrinthine alleys, Arthur's mind drifted to the supernatural horrors he had faced in the past. The memory of a particularly harrowing encounter with a malevolent spirit in Whitechapel sent a shiver down his spine. He paused, leaning against a damp brick wall, his breath misting in the cold air.

"Am I truly prepared for what lies ahead?" he whispered, doubt creeping into his voice. "The dangers I've faced before... they pale in comparison to what Thornhill might unleash."

Arthur closed his eyes, allowing himself a moment of vulnerability. The weight of his responsibility pressed down upon him, a burden he had carried for years but never felt more acutely than now. When he opened his eyes again, they held a steely resolve.

"It matters not," he said firmly. "Evelyn's life hangs in the balance. My fears, my doubts—they must be set aside. I must press on for her sake and the sake of all, London."

With renewed determination, Arthur pushed himself off the wall. He continued his journey into the heart of the fogbound city, ready to confront whatever horrors awaited him in the shadows.

Arthur Blackwood's mind raced as he strode purposefully through the fog-shrouded streets of London. His footsteps echoed off the cobblestones, a steady rhythm that matched the pounding of his heart. He pulled his coat tighter around him, more out of habit than for warmth, as his thoughts coalesced into a plan.

"Thornhill's obsession with the occult," he muttered to himself, "it's the key. He wouldn't risk taking Evelyn to any common hideout. No, he'd seek a place of power."

Arthur's piercing blue eyes scanned the mist-laden surroundings, his intuition heightened by years of supernatural investigations. He paused at a crossroads, the gas lamps casting eerie, elongated shadows across the pavement.

"The old Blackfriar's Monastery," he breathed, a spark of realization igniting in his mind. "Of course. Its dark history would appeal to Thornhill's twisted sensibilities."

As Arthur resumed his journey, the fog seemed to thicken, wrapping around him like a suffocating shroud. The air grew heavy, laden with an oppressive silence that pressed against his ears. He could feel the weight of unseen eyes upon him, watching from the shadows.

"This fog," he whispered, his voice barely audible, "it's unnatural. Thornhill's influence grows stronger."

A distant clock tower chimed for the hour, its mournful tones distorted by the mist. Arthur quickened his pace, his determination mounting with each step. The atmosphere seemed to resist his progress, the fog swirling around his legs as if trying to impede his movement.

"Hold on, Evelyn," he murmured, his jaw set with grim resolve. "I'm coming for you, no matter what dark forces stand in my way."

Arthur approached a dimly lit tavern, its weathered sign creaking in the damp night air.

He hesitated, his hand hovering over the door handle. The establishment was known to harbor informants and those who might betray him to the Order. Steeling himself, he pushed open the door and entered.

The tavern's interior was thick with pipe smoke and hushed conversations. Arthur made his way to the bar, his eyes constantly scanning the room. The bartender, a grizzled man with a scar across his left cheek, eyed him warily.

"What'll it be, guv'nor?" he growled.

"Information," Arthur replied quietly, sliding a coin across the bar. "About Reginald Thornhill."

The bartender's eyes narrowed. "Dangerous name to be throwing about, that is."

Arthur leaned in closer, his voice barely above a whisper. "I'm well aware of the risks. But a life hangs in the balance."

A tense silence stretched between them. Arthur could feel his heart pounding, acutely aware of every subtle movement in the tavern. Finally, the bartender jerked his head towards a shadowy corner.

"Try old Maggie over there. But mind yourself—she's as like to help as she is to slit your throat."

Arthur nodded his thanks and made his way to the indicated table. An elderly woman sat hunched over a glass of gin, her rheumy eyes fixed on the swirling liquid.

"Maggie?" Arthur asked cautiously, taking a seat across from her.

The woman's gaze snapped up, surprisingly sharp. "Who's asking?"

"Someone in need of your... unique insights," Arthur replied, choosing his words carefully.

"About Reginald Thornhill and the Order of the Eternal Flame."

Maggie hissed, her gnarled fingers tightening around her glass. "Fool! You'll bring their wrath down upon us all!"

Arthur leaned forward, his voice low and urgent. "A woman's life is at stake. Please, any information could be crucial."

Maggie studied him for a long moment, her eyes seeming to pierce through to his very soul.

Finally, she spoke, her voice a raspy whisper.

"The old Blackfriar's Monastery. That's where you'll find your man. But beware, detective. The veil between worlds grows thin there, and dark forces gather."

Arthur felt a chill run down his spine but pushed aside his unease. "Thank you, Maggie. Your help won't be forgotten."

As he stood to leave, Maggie grabbed his wrist with surprising strength. "Take this," she pressed a small, worn amulet into his palm. "For protection. You'll need all you can get where you're going."

Arthur nodded solemnly, pocketing the amulet.

As he stepped back into the fog-shrouded streets, his mind raced. The Blackfriar's Monastery—his intuition had been correct. But what horrors awaited him there? And would he be in time to save Evelyn from whatever dark ritual Thornhill had planned?

With renewed determination, Arthur set off into the night, the weight of the amulet a constant reminder of the supernatural dangers that lay ahead.

Arthur Blackwood's footsteps echoed on the damp cobblestones as he strode purposefully through the fog-laden streets of London. His piercing blue eyes scanned the murky surroundings, ever vigilant for any sign of pursuit or ambush. The weight of Maggie's amulet pressed against his chest, a constant reminder of the otherworldly perils that awaited him.

"Evelyn," he murmured under his breath, his voice tinged with a mixture of concern and determination. "I'm coming for you, come hell or high water."

As he rounded a corner, a shadowy figure darted across his path, causing Arthur to reach for his revolver instinctively. The figure dissolved into the mist, leaving him questioning whether it had been real or merely a trick of the light.

"Steady on, old boy," he chided himself. "Can't go jumping at every shadow."

Yet even as he attempted to calm his nerves, Arthur's mind raced with possibilities. What if Thornhill had set a trap? What if he was walking into an ambush? The detective shook his head, banishing such thoughts. Evelyn needed him, and he would not falter now.

As the looming silhouette of the old Blackfriar's Monastery emerged from the fog, Arthur felt a chill run down his spine that had nothing to do with the damp night air. The decrepit structure seemed to exude an aura of malevolence, its crumbling stonework a stark reminder of the passage of time and its secrets.

"Right then," Arthur muttered, steeling himself. "Into the lion's den, we go."

With a deep breath, he approached the iron-bound oak door, its surface marred by arcane symbols that seemed to writhe in the flickering gaslight. As he reached for the handle, a sudden gust of wind extinguished the nearby streetlamps, plunging him into near-total darkness.

Arthur's hand hovered over the door, his heart pounding in his chest. Whatever lay beyond, he knew, would change everything. With a silent prayer, he grasped the handle. He pushed, the ancient hinges groaning in protest as the door swung open to reveal the yawning darkness within.

Arthur stepped across the threshold, the floorboards creaking ominously beneath his feet. The musty air inside the monastery assaulted his senses, carrying with it the faint scent of incense and something far more sinister.

"Evelyn?" he called out softly, his voice echoing in the cavernous space. No response came save for the skittering of unseen vermin in the shadows.

As his eyes adjusted to the gloom, Arthur withdrew a small oil lamp from his coat pocket. With practiced ease, he lit it, casting a warm glow that barely penetrated the oppressive darkness.

"Steady on, old boy," he murmured to himself.

"One step at a time."

The detective's mind raced as he cautiously advanced deeper into the monastery. What horrors had Evelyn endured at the hands of Thornhill and his twisted followers? The thought of her suffering fueled his determination, even as it threatened to overwhelm him with dread.

A sudden noise from above caused Arthur to freeze in his tracks. His free hand instinctively moved to the revolver concealed beneath his coat.

"Who's there?" he demanded, his voice steady despite the hammering of his heart. "Show yourself!"

Silence answered him, broken only by the gentle hiss of his lamp's flame. Arthur's eyes darted about, searching for any sign of movement in the shadows. He couldn't shake the feeling that unseen eyes were watching his every move.

"Focus, Blackwood," he chided himself internally. "Your intuition has never led you astray before. Trust it now."

With renewed resolve, Arthur pressed on, his senses heightened to a razor's edge. Each step brought him closer to unraveling the mystery of the Order of the Eternal Flame and to Evelyn. Whatever challenges lay ahead, he would face them head-on, for her sake and for the sake of justice.

As he approached a heavy curtain at the far end of the hall, Arthur paused, his hand hovering inches from the fabric. Beyond this veil, he knew, lay answers—and quite possibly, mortal danger. Drawing a deep breath, he steeled himself for what was to come.

"Into the abyss," Arthur whispered, his voice barely audible. With a swift motion, he pulled back the curtain, ready to confront whatever secrets the monastery held within its ancient walls.

Chapter 14: Resurrection

The flickering gaslight cast long shadows across Detective Arthur Blackwood's study, illuminating the scattered papers and cryptic notes that littered his desk. His piercing blue eyes darted from one clue to the next, his mind racing as he pieced together the final elements of his plan. The Shadowmaster's lair, Evelyn's captivity, and the Order's dark rituals swirled together in a murky tapestry of conspiracy and occult machinations.

Blackwood's fingers trembled slightly as he traced a line between two seemingly unconnected pieces of evidence. "The old Underground station," he murmured. "Of course. Hidden in plain sight, yet cloaked in shadow."

He paused, doubt gnawing at the edges of his resolve. How often had he followed false leads down foggy alleyways, only to find himself trapped in the Shadowmaster's web of deception? The weight of his failures pressed down upon him, threatening to crush his spirit.

"No," Blackwood growled, clenching his fist. "I cannot falter now. Evelyn's life hangs in the balance."

He closed his eyes, drawing in a deep breath.

When he opened them again, a steely determination had replaced the uncertainty in his gaze.

"I've come too far to turn back," he declared to the empty room. "Whatever traps await, whatever horrors I must face - I will see this through to the bitter end."

Blackwood's mind raced ahead, envisioning the labyrinthine tunnels beneath London's streets. He could almost feel the damp chill of the underground and hear the distant drip of water echoing through abandoned corridors.

"The Order thinks themselves beyond the reach of justice," he mused, a grim smile playing at the corners of his mouth. "But they have never faced a foe quite like me. I've stared into the abyss and returned. What terrors can they conjure that I have not already conquered?"

With renewed purpose, Blackwood gathered the most crucial pieces of evidence, committing their details to memory. Time was of the essence - he could feel it slipping away with each tick of the ornate clock on his mantle.

"Hold on, Evelyn," he whispered. "I'm coming for you. And as for you, Lord Ashford - your reign of shadows ends tonight."

Blackwood moved with practiced efficiency, his lean frame bending and stretching as he methodically prepared for the impending confrontation. He reached for a worn leather satchel, its contents rattling softly as he set it on his desk.

"Silver bullets," he murmured, checking the chambers of his revolver with deft fingers. "Holy water, iron filings, and..." He paused, withdrawing a small vial filled with a viscous, dark liquid. "Shadowbane essence. May it prove as potent as the legends claim."

As he secured each item about his person, Blackwood's thoughts turned inward. "How many times have I stood on the precipice of the unknown?" he pondered. "Yet never has the stakes been so high, nor the foe so formidable."

The air in the study suddenly chilled, a familiar presence materializing behind him. Blackwood turned, his piercing blue eyes meeting the ethereal form of Lady Eleanor Ravenscroft.

"Arthur," her voice echoed, tinged with urgency and compassion. "The hour grows late. Are you prepared for what lies ahead?"

Blackwood squared his shoulders, his jaw set with determination. "As prepared as one can be when facing the darkness, my lady. Your counsel has been invaluable, but I fear this is a path I must walk alone."

Lady Ravenscroft's spectral form shimmered, and her expression mixed sorrow and resolve.

"You may walk alone, dear Arthur, but you do not stand alone. The spirits of those wronged by The Shadowmaster's machinations rally behind you."

"I am grateful for their support," Blackwood replied, his voice low and measured. "But tell me, Lady Eleanor, what awaits me in the depths of the Order's sanctum? What horrors must I face to rescue Evelyn?"

The ghost's eyes clouded as if peering into a realm beyond mortal comprehension.

"Shadows within shadows, Arthur. Creatures are born of nightmares and fed by fear. But remember - your greatest weapon is not the tools you carry, but the light of truth that burns within you."

Blackwood nodded solemnly, absorbing her words. "And what of Lord Ashford? Will I find him there, puppeteering his dark designs?"

"He is there," Lady Ravenscroft confirmed, her voice hardening. "But be wary, Arthur. The man you knew is but a shell, consumed by the very power he sought to control. He is The Shadowmaster now, in body and spirit."

"Then it ends tonight," Blackwood declared, his hand instinctively tightening around the grip of his revolver. "One way or another, I will put an end to this madness."

Lady Ravenscroft's form began to fade, her final words hanging in the air like mist.

"Remember, Arthur - even the faintest light can guide the way in the darkest night. Go now, with our blessings, and may you return victorious."

As her presence dissipated, Blackwood felt a surge of renewed purpose course through him.

He cast one final glance around his study, committing to memory the sanctuary of knowledge and reason he might never see again.

"Into the abyss," he whispered, striding towards the door with unwavering resolve. "For Evelyn, for justice, and for all those who have fallen victim to the shadows."

Detective Arthur Blackwood stepped out into the fog-laden streets of London, the chill air biting at his exposed skin. The gas lamps struggled to penetrate the thick, swirling mist that enveloped the city like a ghostly shroud. As he moved purposefully through the eerie veil, his footsteps muffled on the damp cobblestones, Blackwood's mind raced with thoughts of the impending confrontation.

"The Shadowmaster awaits," he muttered to himself, his breath visible in the frigid night. "And with him, the fate of Evelyn and perhaps all of London."

Blackwood's senses heightened as he navigated the labyrinthine streets, and every shadow and sound amplified in the oppressive silence. The distant clop of horse hooves echoed ominously, seeming to come from all directions simultaneously.

Suddenly, a dark figure emerged from the fog ahead, causing Blackwood to be tense. His hand instinctively moved towards his concealed revolver.

"Who goes there?" he called out, his voice steady despite the hammering of his heart.

The figure stepped closer, revealing itself as nothing more than a weary lamplighter making his rounds. Blackwood relaxed slightly but remained alert.

"Nasty night for a stroll, sir," the lamplighter remarked, peering at Blackwood curiously.

"Best be careful. Strange things afoot in this fog, they say."

Blackwood nodded grimly. "Indeed. Keep to the light, my good man. The shadows hold more danger than you know."

As the lamplighter moved on, Blackwood's thoughts turned inward. "How many innocents like him are unaware of the malevolence that lurks beyond their perception? The Order's tendrils reach far, and Ashford's ambition knows no bounds."

He pressed on, his intuition guiding him through the maze-like streets. Every rustle of fabric, every distant cry, set his nerves on edge.

The weight of his mission pressed down upon him, as heavy as the fog that surrounded him.

"I must not falter now," Blackwood whispered to himself, steeling his resolve. "Too much depends on this night's outcome."

Blackwood halted before an imposing iron gate, its twisted bars adorned with arcane symbols that seemed to writhe in the dim gaslight. The entrance to the Order's sanctum loomed before him, a bastion of darkness against the fog-shrouded night. He drew a deep breath, steadying his nerves as he placed a hand upon the cold metal.

"For Evelyn," he murmured, his voice barely audible. "For justice."

His fingers trembled slightly as he withdrew a small, ornate key from his waistcoat pocket. The weight of his task bore down upon him, threatening to crush his resolve. But as he inserted the key into the lock, a steely determination settled over his features.

"I've come too far to falter now," Blackwood thought, his jaw set. "The Shadowmaster's reign of terror ends tonight."

With a resounding click, the gate swung open, revealing a narrow courtyard beyond.

Blackwood stepped through, his senses heightened to a knife's edge. The sanctum's facade rose before him, a Gothic horror of stone and shadow.

As he approached the entrance, a chill ran down his spine. "What devilry awaits within?" he wondered, his hand instinctively moving to the revolver concealed beneath his coat.

Blackwood pushed the heavy oak door open, wincing at the creak that shattered the eerie silence. He stepped inside, immediately enveloped by an oppressive atmosphere that seemed to press against his soul.

"By God," he whispered, his eyes straining to adjust to the gloom. "What unholy presence resides here?"

His footsteps echoed unnaturally as he moved down the dimly lit corridor, each sound reverberating off the stone walls. Blackwood's heart pounded in his chest, a staccato rhythm that seemed to count down the moments until his inevitable confrontation with the Order's inner circle.

"Steady on, old boy," he reassured himself, fighting to maintain his composure. "Evelyn needs you. London needs you."

As he ventured deeper into the sanctum's depths, Blackwood couldn't shake the feeling that unseen eyes were watching his every move. The weight of centuries of arcane knowledge and forbidden rituals seemed to hang in the air, threatening to smother him with their evil intent.

"Whatever horrors you've conjured, Thornhill," Blackwood thought grimly, "I'll see them undone. For the sake of all that is good and just in this world."

As Blackwood advanced deeper into the sanctum, the flickering gas lamps cast writhing shadows on the walls. He paused, his keen senses alert to every subtle shift in the air. A barely audible whisper brushed past his ear, causing him to whirl around.

"Who's there?" he demanded, his voice low and taut.

Nothing but silence answered him, yet the hair on the back of his neck stood on end.

Blackwood's blue eyes narrowed as he scanned the corridor, his hand never straying far from his concealed revolver.

"Trickery and illusion," he muttered to himself.

"Focus, Arthur. Remember what's at stake."

As if in response to his thoughts, a shadow detached itself from the wall, slithering across the floor with unnatural speed. Blackwood's heart leapt into his throat, but he forced himself to remain still, watching as the shadow dissolved into nothingness.

"By heaven," he breathed, "what manner of dark arts are at work here?"

Steeling himself, Blackwood pressed on, each step measured and deliberate. The whispers grew more insistent, a cacophony of unintelligible murmurs that seemed to come from everywhere and nowhere.

At last, he arrived at a heavy iron-bound door, ornate symbols etched into its surface.

Blackwood's intuition, honed by years of confronting the unexplainable, told him that Evelyn lay beyond.

"Hold fast, Miss Bradshaw," he thought, his jaw set with determination. "I'm coming for you."

Pressing his ear to the door, Blackwood listened intently, his breath held. For a moment, only silence greeted him. Then, faintly, he heard the rustle of fabric and a muffled voice.

"Evelyn," he whispered, his heart pounding with anticipation. "Pray God I'm not too late."

Detective Arthur Blackwood's mind raced, piecing together the fragments of information he'd gathered. Evelyn's presence confirmed, he now faced the daunting task of extracting her from the clutches of Reginald Thornhill and his nefarious cohorts.

"Three guards, at least," Blackwood muttered, his piercing blue eyes darting about as he formulated a plan. "Thornhill's likely armed, and who knows what arcane defenses he's erected."

He reached into his coat, his fingers brushing against a small vial. A memory flashed—Lady Eleanor's spirit, her words echoing in his mind: "When darkness threatens to overwhelm, let this light be your guide."

Blackwood's lips curved into a grim smile. "Very well, old girl. Let's see what your little concoction can do."

With practiced ease, he uncorked the vial and poured its contents onto the door's hinges. A faint sizzling sound reached his ears as the liquid ate through the metal.

"Now, for a distraction," he thought, reaching for a small, egg-shaped device in his pocket.

Blackwood took a deep breath, steeling himself for what was to come. "Once more unto the breach," he whispered, then kicked the door open with a resounding crack.

In one fluid motion, he tossed the device into the room. A blinding flash erupted, followed by billowing smoke. Cries of confusion and alarm filled the air.

"What in blazes?" Thornhill's voice rang out, laced with fury and fear.

Blackwood surged forward, his intuition guiding him through the chaos. He caught sight of a figure stumbling blindly—one of the guards.

With precise movements, he incapacitated the man with a sharp blow to the head.

"Evelyn!" Blackwood called out, his voice cutting through the din. "Where are you?"

"Arthur!" came the reply, strained but unmistakable. "Here, by the far wall!"

Dodging grasping hands and flailing limbs, Blackwood approached her voice. His heart pounded in his chest, every sense on high alert.

"Stop him, you fools!" Thornhill bellowed, his composure shattered.

Blackwood's hand found Evelyn's arm, and he pulled her close. "Hold tight," he instructed, his voice low and urgent. "We're getting out of here."

As they moved towards the exit, Blackwood's keen ears caught the sound of a pistol being cocked. Without hesitation, he spun, placing himself between Evelyn and the perceived threat.

"Not so fast, Detective," Thornhill's voice cut through the thinning, cold, menacing smoke. "I'm afraid your meddling ends here."

With Evelyn safely at his side, Blackwood felt relief wash over him. He turned to her, his piercing blue eyes meeting her determined gaze. In the dim light of the sanctum, her face was pale but resolute.

"Are you hurt?" he asked, his voice low and urgent.

Evelyn shook her head, a wry smile playing at the corners of her mouth. "Nothing that won't heal, Arthur. Your timing, as always, is impeccable."

Blackwood allowed himself a brief chuckle, the tension in his shoulders easing slightly. "I'm glad you approve, Miss Bradshaw. Though I fear our ordeal is far from over."

"Indeed," Evelyn replied, her tone growing serious. "The Shadowmaster—"

"—is still at large," Blackwood finished, his mind already racing ahead. "And we must stop him before he can complete whatever nefarious ritual he has planned."

Evelyn's eyes flashed with determination. "Then let's not waste another moment. I didn't endure Thornhill's tedious monologuing just to falter at the final hurdle."

Blackwood nodded, impressed once again by her resilience. "Your courage never ceases to amaze me, Evelyn. Are you certain you're ready for what lies ahead?"

"As ready as one can be when facing an occult mastermind," she quipped, then added more softly, "But with you by my side, I believe we stand a fighting chance."

The detective felt a warmth bloom in his chest at her words. "Then let us proceed," he said, drawing his revolver. "Stay close, and be on your guard. The Shadowmaster's tricks are as devious as they are deadly."

Together, they moved deeper into the sanctum, their footsteps echoing off the stone walls. The air grew thick with an oppressive energy that seemed to pulse with malevolent intent. Blackwood's intuition prickled, warning him of unseen dangers lurking in the shadows.

As they approached a grand archway adorned with arcane symbols, Blackwood paused, his hand instinctively reaching out to halt Evelyn.

"Wait," he whispered, his eyes narrowing as he studied the glyphs. "There's something not quite right here."

Evelyn leaned in, her breath warm against his ear. "What do you see, Arthur?"

"A trap," he murmured, his mind working furiously to decipher the cryptic markings. "But also... a clue. The Shadowmaster's hubris may yet be his undoing."

With bated breath and hearts pounding, they stood on the precipice of their final confrontation, the air crackling with anticipation and the promise of revelations.

Chapter 15: Confrontation

Detective Arthur Blackwood pressed his back against the cold stone wall, his breath forming wispy tendrils in the frigid air of the Order's sanctum. The oppressive silence weighed upon him like a shroud as he inched forward, every nerve attuned to the slightest disturbance. His fingers brushed the rough-hewn surface, seeking purchase in the darkness.

"Steady now, Arthur," he whispered to himself, his voice barely audible. "One misstep could spell disaster."

As he rounded a corner, a faint phosphorescent glow caught his eye. Arcane symbols etched deep into the walls pulsed with an otherworldly light. Blackwood's breath caught in his throat as he recognized their sinister nature.

"By God," he murmured, examining the eldritch markings. "These are the very sigils described in the Codex Umbra. But to see them manifested thus..."

A chill ran down his spine, and Blackwood found himself transported back to that fateful night in Whitechapel when he'd first glimpsed the terrible power such symbols could unleash.

He shook his head, forcing the memory away.

"Focus, man," he chided himself. "The answers you seek lie ahead, not in the past."

Yet as he traced the contours of a particularly malevolent glyph, Blackwood couldn't shake the feeling that he was being watched. The shadows seemed to deepen around him as if reaching out with grasping tendrils.

"I've come too far to turn back now," he thought, steeling his resolve. "Whatever horrors await, I must press on. For Evelyn's sake and for all of London."

With a deep breath, Blackwood tore his gaze from the arcane symbols and continued his cautious advance into the heart of the Order's lair, each step carrying him closer to the truth and danger.

A piercing cry shattered the oppressive silence, echoing through the sanctum's winding corridors. Blackwood's heart leapt into his throat, recognizing the unmistakable timbre of Evelyn's voice.

"Evelyn!" he whispered urgently, his measured pace quickening to a desperate sprint. The Detective's lean frame moved with fluid grace, each step propelled by an overwhelming need to reach her.

As he ran, Blackwood's mind raced. "Hold on, Evelyn. I'm coming," he thought, his jaw clenched with determination. The weight of their shared experiences, the horrors they'd faced together, fueled his resolve.

Rounding a final corner, Blackwood burst into a grand chamber that took his breath away. At its center stood an imposing altar adorned with arcane artifacts that seemed to pulse with malevolent energy. But it was the figures flanking the altar that truly arrested his attention.

Lord Percival Ashford, the Shadowmaster himself, cut an imperious figure. His silver-streaked hair and impeccable attire belied the darkness lurking in his piercing blue eyes. Beside him stood Reginald Thornhill, his sharp features twisted into a smirk of cruel satisfaction.

"Ah, Detective Blackwood," Lord Ashford's cultured voice dripped with false cordiality.

"How kind of you to join us for this momentous occasion."

Blackwood's hand instinctively moved towards his concealed revolver, but he refrained, knowing he was outmatched. Instead, he met Ashford's gaze steadily, his own blue eyes blazing with defiance.

"Where is she, Ashford?" Blackwood demanded, his voice low and dangerous.

Thornhill chuckled, a sound devoid of mirth.

"Your precious Evelyn is quite safe, I assure you. For now."

Blackwood's mind raced as he assessed the situation. The chamber's oppressive atmosphere and a palpable sense of otherworldly power pointed to a ritual on the verge of completion, and he had to act quickly.

"Whatever you're planning, Ashford, it ends here," Blackwood declared, taking a step forward. "You cannot hope to control the forces you're toying with."

Lord Ashford's lips curled into a cold smile. "Oh, but I can, Detective. And I will. The power of the Eternal Flame will be mine to command, and all of London shall tremble before me."

Blackwood felt the weight of countless lives hanging in the balance as the two men locked eyes across the chamber. He knew that his next move would determine not just Evelyn's fate but the future of the entire city he'd sworn to protect.

Blackwood's jaw clenched, his piercing gaze never wavering from Lord Ashford's smug countenance. "You speak of power, Ashford, but you've no concept of the devastation you'll unleash," he growled, his voice echoing in the cavernous chamber.

Lord Ashford's laughter rang out, cold and mirthless. "Oh, come now, Detective. Surely a man of your... unique experiences can appreciate the magnitude of what we're about to achieve."

Blackwood's mind raced, recalling the arcane symbols he'd encountered on his way here. The pieces were falling into place, and the picture they formed was chilling. "You're not just seeking power," he realized aloud, "you're attempting to bridge the gap between our world and the realm of shadows."

Reginald Thornhill stepped forward, his dark eyes glinting with ambition. "Perceptive as always, Blackwood," he said, his voice smooth as silk yet laced with venom. "But you fail to see the greater good. Think of the knowledge we'll gain, the advancements we'll make!"

"At what cost?" Blackwood retorted, his fists clenching at his sides. "I've seen firsthand the horrors that lurk beyond the veil. You're playing with forces you can't possibly control."

As Thornhill opened his mouth to reply, Blackwood cut him off. "And don't pretend this is about the greater good, Thornhill. I know about the missing persons and the rituals performed in the shadows of Whitechapel.

You've left a trail of blood and suffering in your wake."

A flicker of surprise crossed Thornhill's face, quickly masked by a sneer. "Sacrifices must be made for progress, Detective. Surely a man of your intellect can understand that."

Blackwood felt a surge of righteous anger course through him. These men, with their delusions of grandeur, were willing to sacrifice innocent lives for their own gain. He had to find a way to stop them, save Evelyn, and prevent the catastrophe they were about to unleash upon London.

"Your 'progress' ends here," Blackwood declared, his voice ringing with determination.

"I won't allow you to tear open the fabric of our world for your twisted ambitions."

The tension in the chamber thickened like the fog that cloaked London's streets. A flicker of movement caught Blackwood's eye, and his heart clenched as Evelyn was dragged into view. Her wrists were bound with coarse rope, angry red marks visible where she had struggled against her bonds. Yet, despite her captivity, her emerald eyes blazed with defiance.

Blackwood's gaze locked with hers, a silent exchange passing between them. In that fleeting moment, he saw her strength, her unwavering resolve. He felt a swell of admiration and a fierce protectiveness that steeled his resolve.

"I see our guest of honor has arrived," Lord Ashford drawled, his aristocratic tones dripping with false cordiality. "Miss Bradshaw has been most... uncooperative in our efforts to enlighten her."

Evelyn's chin lifted, her voice sharp as a razor. What you think is wisdom is just an illusion, Lord Ashford. A facade to mask your lust for power.

Blackwood watched as The Shadowmaster's eyes narrowed, a flicker of genuine respect—or was it fear?—crossing his features. He turned to Blackwood, his demeanor shifting.

"Detective Blackwood," Lord Ashford purred, "surely a man of your... unique experiences can appreciate the potential here. Think of the mysteries we could unravel together, the barriers we could break."

Blackwood felt a chill run down his spine, recognizing the seductive pull of forbidden knowledge. For a heartbeat, he allowed himself to imagine it—the secrets of the universe laid bare before him. But then he remembered the cost, the faces of those who had fallen victim to such temptations.

"No," Blackwood said, his voice low but unwavering. "I've seen where that path leads, Lord Ashford. It ends in madness and destruction. My allegiance is to justice, to protecting the innocent from men like you who would sacrifice them for their own gain."

Lord Ashford's mask of civility slipped, revealing a flash of the darkness that lurked beneath. "How disappointingly predictable," he sneered. "I had hoped you might prove more... adaptable."

Blackwood's hand inched towards the revolver concealed beneath his coat. "The only adaptation you need concern yourself with, Lord Ashford," he said, his voice hard as steel, "is how you'll fare in a prison cell."

A sudden tremor shook the chamber as Blackwood's words hung in the air. The Detective's eyes darted around, his senses heightened by years of confronting the inexplicable. The very air seemed to thicken, crackling with an unseen energy that made the hairs on the back of his neck stand on end.

"You fool," Lord Ashford hissed, his aristocratic facade crumbling. "You've no idea what forces you're trifling with."

Blackwood's mind raced, recalling similar manifestations he'd witnessed in haunted manors and cursed crypts. This was different, more potent. He planted his feet firmly, bracing against the malevolent tide that threatened to overwhelm him.

"Evelyn," he called out, his voice steady despite the supernatural maelstrom building around them. "Whatever happens, stay behind me!"

The journalist's eyes widened, but she nodded, her own resolve evident. "Arthur, the symbols on the floor—they're glowing!"

Indeed, the arcane markings etched into the stone pulsed with otherworldly light. Lord Ashford raised his arms, his voice echoing an inhuman quality as he intoned words in a language long dead.

Blackwood's hand closed around the cold iron of his revolver, knowing its limited use against what was coming. "I've faced your kind before, Ashford," he growled. "Your parlor tricks don't impress me."

The Shadowmaster's laughter reverberated unnaturally. "Oh, but these are no mere tricks, Detective. Behold the true power of the Order!"

With a gesture, swirling masses of shadow coalesced into vaguely humanoid shapes.

Wraiths, Blackwood realized, his blood running cold. Spirits of the vengeful dead twisted to Ashford's will.

Blackwood's mind raced through every scrap of occult knowledge he'd gleaned over the years as the ethereal monstrosities surged toward him. Iron repelled some spirits, salt others. But these... these were something else entirely.

"Stay back!" he shouted, firing a round at the nearest wraith. The bullet passed harmlessly through its shadowy form.

Blackwood pivoted, using his body to shield Evelyn as a wraith's clawed hand swiped at them. He felt an unnatural chill graze his coat.

"Arthur!" Evelyn cried out. "How do we fight them?"

"We can't," Blackwood grunted, dodging another attack. "Not directly. But every summoning has a source. We need to disrupt whatever's anchoring them to this plane."

Blackwood's eyes scanned the chamber as he spoke, searching for anything that might be the focal point of Ashford's ritual. The altar? The glowing symbols? Or perhaps...

His gaze locked onto the ornate ring adorning Lord Ashford's finger, pulsing with the same eerie light as the floor markings. Blackwood's intuition, honed by countless supernatural encounters, screamed that this was the key.

"Evelyn," he whispered urgently, "I need a distraction. Can you manage it?"

Her eyes gleamed with understanding. "Leave it to me, Detective. I didn't become London's most notorious journalist by being shy."

With that, she launched into a tirade of insults and accusations at Lord Ashford, each barb carefully crafted to wound his considerable ego. As the Shadowmaster's attention wavered, Blackwood saw his chance.

He lunged forward, dodging wraiths and making straight for Ashford. The aristocrat's eyes widened in shock as Blackwood closed the distance between them.

"This ends now!" Blackwood roared, grappling for the ring.

Blackwood's fingers closed around the ring, its surface burning cold against his skin. With a forceful twist, he wrenched it from Lord Ashford's hand. The Shadowmaster let out an inhuman howl of rage and pain.

"No!" Ashford screamed, his composure shattering. "You fool! You'll destroy us all!"

Blackwood paid him no heed, his piercing blue eyes fixed on the altar. He hurled the ring towards the stone surface with every ounce of strength.

"Evelyn, get down!" he shouted, diving to shield her as the ring struck the altar.

A blinding flash erupted, followed by a deafening crack that shook the very foundations of the chamber. The air itself seemed to ripple, dark energy dissipating like smoke in a strong wind. The wraiths' unearthly shrieks faded, their spectral forms unraveling before Blackwood's eyes.

Blackwood's keen ears caught the sound of hurried footsteps as the chaos subsided. He whirled around to see Reginald Thornhill, his face a mask of panic, making a desperate dash for the chamber's exit.

"Oh no, you don't," Blackwood muttered, his voice low and determined. With the agility of a seasoned detective, he sprang into action, cutting off Thornhill's escape route.

Thornhill's eyes darted wildly, like a cornered animal. "Blackwood, be reasonable," he pleaded, his usual eloquence abandoning him. "You don't understand the forces at play here. We were trying to—"

"Save your breath, Thornhill," Blackwood interrupted, his tone sharp as he advanced.

"Your machinations end here."

Thornhill lunged suddenly, attempting to slip past, but Blackwood was ready. He pivoted, using Thornhill's momentum against him, and grappled the man to the ground. They struggled fiercely, Thornhill's desperation lending him strength, but Blackwood's years of experience proved the deciding factor.

With Thornhill subdued and the supernatural threat neutralized, Blackwood turned his attention to the true architect of this dark design. Lord Percival Ashford, the Shadowmaster, stood at the chamber's far end, his aristocratic features etched with fury and disbelief.

"It's over, Ashford," Blackwood declared, his piercing blue eyes locked on the nobleman.

"Your ritual has failed, and your pawns have scattered."

The Shadowmaster's lips curled into a sneer.

"You understand nothing, Detective. The power I sought... it would have reshaped the very fabric of our world."

Blackwood felt a chill run down his spine but kept his voice steady. "At what cost? The lives of innocents? The very soul of London?"

"Sacrifices are necessary for greatness," Ashford retorted, his tone dripping with condescension.

"I would have ushered in an era of unparalleled knowledge and power. The Order of the Eternal Flame would have ruled from the shadows, guiding humanity to its true potential."

As Ashford spoke, Blackwood's mind raced. The man's ambition was staggering, bordering on madness. He thought of the victims he'd seen, the terror that had gripped the city. "And you'd build this new world on a foundation of blood and suffering?" he asked, disgust evident in his voice.

The Shadowmaster's eyes gleamed with fanatical zeal. "You're short-sighted, Blackwood. In time, you would have seen the wisdom of our actions."

Blackwood squared his shoulders, his resolve hardening. "I've seen enough, Ashford. Here's what will happen: you will dissolve the Order immediately. And you will release Miss Bradshaw unharmed."

"Or what, detective?" Ashford scoffed, though Blackwood noticed a flicker of uncertainty in his eyes.

"Or I'll ensure that every sordid detail of your 'Order' finds its way to the proper authorities - and the press," Blackwood countered, his voice low and dangerous. "I wonder how your aristocratic peers would react to learning of your dabblings in the occult? How long would your power last once exposed to the light of day?"

He could see the realization dawning on Ashford's face, the carefully constructed facade of control crumbling. The Shadowmaster's shoulders sagged, the fight draining out of him.

"You've won this round, Blackwood," Ashford muttered, his voice barely above a whisper.

"But mark my words, the hunger for power that drives men like me... it will never truly be extinguished."

As Blackwood watched the once-mighty Shadowmaster capitulate, he felt no triumph, only a bone-deep weariness. The battle was won, but he knew the war against the darkness that lurked in the hearts of men would never truly end.

The sanctum's oppressive atmosphere seemed to lift as Blackwood and Evelyn walked through the winding corridors. The flickering gaslight cast long shadows on the damp stone walls.

Blackwood's keen senses remained alert, his body tense with the lingering threat of danger.

"Are you alright, Miss Bradshaw?" he asked, his voice low and tinged with concern.

Evelyn nodded, her chin held high despite the ordeal. "I'm quite well, Detective. Though I must admit, this is one story I hadn't anticipated uncovering when I began my investigation."

A ghost of a smile played on Blackwood's lips.

"Indeed. Your tenacity is admirable, if somewhat reckless."

They paused at a junction, and Blackwood studied Evelyn's face. The determination in her eyes mirrored his own, and he felt a sudden kinship with this intrepid journalist.

"You've seen things tonight that most would scarcely believe," Blackwood said softly, his mind racing with the implications of the evening's events. "What will you do with this knowledge?"

Evelyn's gaze met his, unwavering. "The truth must be told, Detective. No matter how fantastical or frightening. We must shed light on the darkness, is it not?"

Blackwood nodded a mixture of admiration and trepidation coursing through him. "It is. But be cautious, Miss Bradshaw. Some would go to great lengths to keep such truths hidden."

As they neared the exit, the fog from the London streets began to seep in, carrying with it the familiar scents of coal smoke and damp earth. Blackwood felt the weight of responsibility settles upon his shoulders once more.

"This is far from over," he mused, more to himself than to Evelyn. "The Order may be dissolved, but the evil it sought to harness still lurks in the shadows of our city."

Evelyn placed a hand on his arm, her touch unexpectedly reassuring. "Then we shall face it together, Detective. Your insight and my pen—a formidable alliance against the darkness, wouldn't you say?"

For the first time that night, Blackwood felt a spark of hope ignite within him. "Indeed, Miss Bradshaw. Indeed."

As they stepped out into the fogbound streets of London, the gas lamps casting a ghostly glow through the mist, Blackwood knew that this was the beginning of a new chapter in his relentless pursuit of earthly and otherworldly justice.

Chapter 16: Climax

The iron-bound door creaked open, revealing a hollow chamber shrouded in darkness.

Detective Arthur Blackwood crossed the threshold, his senses immediately assaulted by an otherworldly chill that permeated the air. As his eyes adjusted to the gloom, he perceived the outlines of ancient stone pillars stretching upward into shadowy vaults above.

"Steady now, old boy," Blackwood muttered to himself, his voice barely above a whisper.

He took a cautious step forward, the tap of his boot echoing ominously in the vast space. An unseen presence seemed to press upon him from all sides as if the very walls were alive with evil intent. Blackwood's hand instinctively moved to the revolver concealed beneath his coat, though he knew such mundane weapons would be of little use against the spectral forces that dwelt here.

A faint glow caught his eye as he advanced into the chamber. Etched into the stone floor before him was an intricate pattern of arcane symbols pulsing with an eerie blue light.

Blackwood halted, his mind racing as he recalled Agnes O'Reilly's words.

"When faced with the devil's script," her motherly voice echoed in his memory, "tread not on the lines that bind, lest ye be bound yourself, love."

Blackwood's eyes narrowed as he studied the glowing sigils. "Clever," he mused. "A trap for the unwary, no doubt."

He began picking his way across the chamber with painstaking care, placing each foot precisely between the glowing lines. The symbols seemed to flare brighter as he passed, as if in angry protest at being thwarted.

"I do hope you're right about this, Agnes," Blackwood murmured, a bead of sweat trickling down his temple despite the chill. "I've no desire to end up as decoration for this accursed sanctum."

As he neared the center of the room, the weight of unseen gazes grew heavier.

Blackwood's skin crawled with the certainty that he was being observed, judged, perhaps even toyed with by forces beyond mortal ken. He pressed on, steeling his resolve against the rising tide of supernatural dread that threatened to overwhelm him.

"Whatever horrors you have in store," he declared to the oppressive silence, his voice ringing with quiet determination, "know that I will not falter. Too much depends on what I must do here today."

With those words, Blackwood continued his perilous advance into the heart of the Order's lair, each step bringing him closer to a confrontation that would shake the very foundations of his world.

The air grew perceptibly colder as Blackwood approached the central chamber, each exhale forming a ghostly plume before his face.

He paused at the threshold, his hand instinctively tightening around the cold iron charm in his pocket—a talisman against dark forces, gifted to him by a grateful widow whose husband's restless spirit he had laid to rest.

"Steady now, Arthur," he whispered to himself, his piercing blue eyes narrowing as they adjusted to the gloom beyond. "The Shadowmaster awaits."

With a deep breath that did little to quell the hammering of his heart, Blackwood stepped into the chamber. The sight that greeted him sent a fresh wave of cold cascading down his spine.

Lord Percival Ashford stood before an altar festooned with grotesque relics—skulls adorned with occult symbols and candlesticks fashioned from what appeared to be human bone. The Shadowmaster's silver-streaked hair gleamed in the flickering candlelight, his immaculate suit a stark contrast to the macabre surroundings.

As their eyes met, Ashford's lips curled into a smile that never reached his ice-blue gaze.

"Detective Blackwood," he intoned, his cultured voice slicing through the oppressive silence. "How good of you to join us. I trust you found your way through my little welcoming committee without too much trouble?"

Blackwood's mind raced, weighing each word before he spoke. "Lord Ashford," he replied, his tone measured yet edged with steel. "Your hospitality leaves much to be desired."

A chuckle escaped Ashford's lips, devoid of warmth. "Come now, Detective. Surely a man of your... unique experiences can appreciate the necessity of caution in these matters."

"Caution?" Blackwood countered, taking a careful step forward. "Is that what you call unleashing demonic forces upon London?"

Ashford's eyes flashed dangerously. "You speak of things you do not understand, Blackwood.

The power that courses through this chamber—can you not feel it? The potential it holds?"

A palpable wave of hostility swept through the room as if in response to Ashford's words.

Blackwood suppressed a shudder, his intuition screaming that they stood on the precipice of something truly horrific.

"I understand more than you know, Ashford," Blackwood replied, his voice low and intense.

"I've seen the aftermath of your 'potential.' The broken lives, the shattered minds. And I'm here to put an end to it."

Ashford's lips curled into a sardonic smile. "End it? My dear Detective, we've only just begun."

He gestured grandly at the altar behind him.

"What you perceive as destruction is merely the chrysalis of a new world order. One where the veil between realms is torn asunder, and those with the will to grasp power can shape reality itself."

Blackwood's jaw clenched, his eyes never leaving Ashford's face. "You speak of power, but I see only madness. The forces you're toying with cannot be controlled."

"Cannot be controlled?" Ashford's voice dripped with condescension. "That, Detective, is where you and I differ. The weak-minded fear what they cannot understand. But I have peered into the abyss and found it malleable to my will."

As their exchange intensified, Blackwood became acutely aware of a change in the atmosphere. The air grew heavy, charged with an otherworldly energy that made the hairs on the back of his neck stand on end. A chill wind began to stir, whispering through the chamber with an eerie, ethereal quality.

Blackwood's instincts screamed danger. He subtly shifted his stance, ready to move at a moment's notice. "And at what cost, Ashford?"

He pressed, fighting to keep his voice steady.

"How many more must suffer for your ambition?"

The wind picked up, swirling around them with increasing ferocity. Ashford's eyes gleamed with a fanatical light. "Suffering is transient, Detective. I offer eternal power—a new age where the gifted few will rise above the masses."

As Ashford spoke, Blackwood's keen senses detected a change in the shadows cast by the flickering candlelight. They seemed to deepen, to writhe with a life of their own. The Detective's heart raced, knowing that the true battle was about to begin.

A shimmering mist coalesced beside Blackwood, the air rippling as if reality itself was being gently parted. Lady Eleanor Ravenscroft materialized, her ethereal form casting a soft, silvery glow that seemed to push back against the encroaching darkness.

"Arthur," she whispered with a mixture of urgency and compassion. Remember, you do not stand alone in this fight."

Blackwood's breath caught in his throat, a mixture of relief and trepidation washing over him. "Eleanor," he murmured, his piercing blue eyes meeting her spectral gaze. "I feared you might not—"

"I will always come when you need me most," she interjected, a sad smile playing across her translucent features. "Our bond transcends the veil between worlds. Together, we possess the strength to vanquish this evil."

Lord Ashford's laughter cut through their moment of connection, sharp and mocking.

"How touching," he sneered, spreading his arms wide. "The Detective and his ghostly paramour united against the inevitable. Behold, Arthur Blackwood, the true face of power!"

With a gesture that seemed to tear at the very fabric of reality, Ashford called forth the demonic force. The chamber plunged into an unnatural darkness, broken only by veins of sickly green light that pulsed through the air like corrupt arteries.

Blackwood's mind raced, recalling the teachings of the forbidden tome. He could feel Lady Ravenscroft's presence beside him, a beacon of hope amidst the encroaching chaos.

"Now, Arthur!" she urged, her voice having otherworldly resonance. "The incantation—speak it with conviction!"

Drawing a deep breath, Blackwood began to recite the protective spell, his voice growing stronger with each syllable. The words felt heavy on his tongue, ancient and potent. As he spoke, a shimmering barrier began to form around him and Lady Ravenscroft, pushing back against the writhing tendrils of demonic energy.

Ashford's face contorted with rage. "You fool!" he bellowed, his aristocratic veneer crumbling.

"You cannot hope to comprehend, let alone control, such power!"

But Blackwood pressed on, his resolve fortified by Eleanor's unwavering presence. At that moment, surrounded by darkness yet buoyed by an ethereal light, he felt hope. Perhaps they stood a chance against the unholy forces threatening to consume them all.

The chamber erupted into a maelstrom of supernatural forces, the air seeming to ripple and tear as Blackwood and Lady Ravenscroft's combined efforts clashed with the demon's evil power. Blackwood's eyes darted around the room, his senses overwhelmed by the cacophony of unearthly sounds and flashes of eldritch light.

"We must strike at its core, Arthur!" Lady Ravenscroft's voice cut through the chaos, her spectral form flickering like a candle in a storm. "Focus your will upon its essence!"

Blackwood gritted his teeth, sweat beading on his brow as he channeled every ounce of his determination into the struggle. "I'm trying, Eleanor," he growled, his voice strained. "But its influence... it's unlike anything I've encountered before."

A tendril of darkness lashed out, striking Blackwood across the chest and sending him staggering backward. He gasped, feeling as if the very warmth had been sucked from his body.

"Arthur!" Lady Ravenscroft cried out, her ethereal hand reaching for him.

Blackwood's mind reeled dark whispers invading his thoughts. For a moment, despair threatened to overwhelm him. Was this how it would end? All his years of pursuit, only to fail at the final hurdle?

But then he felt a warmth spreading through him, emanating from where Lady Ravenscroft's spectral form overlapped with his own. Her unwavering spirit ignited a renewed vigor within him.

"No," Blackwood muttered, pushing himself to his feet. "I will not yield. Not now, not ever." He locked eyes with Lady Ravenscroft, drawing strength from her resolute gaze. "Together, Eleanor. As one."

With a shared nod of understanding, they redoubled their efforts, Blackwood's incantations melding with Lady Ravenscroft's otherworldly energy. The Detective's voice rose above the din, each word imbued with a power born of unity and determination.

Blackwood's piercing blue eyes locked onto Lady Ravenscroft's ethereal form, their shared gaze a conduit of unspoken understanding. He felt the weight of centuries in her spectral presence, her noble determination flowing through him like quicksilver.

"Now, Eleanor," Blackwood intoned, his voice carrying the gravitas of one who has stared into the abyss and refused to blink. "Let us end this aberration."

Lady Ravenscroft's ghostly visage shimmered with an otherworldly light as she responded, her voice an echo from beyond the veil. "Together, Arthur. Our bond shall be the key."

Blackwood raised his arms, fingers splayed towards the writhing mass of darkness before them. He began to chant, each syllable resonating with power drawn from the depths of his intuition and the strength of their shared purpose.

As the words flowed from his lips, Blackwood's mind raced. 'This is it,' he thought. "All those years of pursuing the supernatural, all those nights poring over arcane tomes—it has led to this moment."

Lady Ravenscroft's form seemed to intertwine with Blackwood's, her spectral energy coursing through him. The chamber trembled, arcane symbols pulsing with an eerie light as the banishment spell took hold.

The demon's form contorted, its unholy screech piercing the air. "You dare?" it bellowed, its voice a cacophony of a thousand tormented souls.

Blackwood gritted his teeth, pushing through the pain that threatened to overwhelm his senses. "I do more than dare," he growled. "I banish you from this realm!"

With a final, thunderous word, Blackwood and Lady Ravenscroft unleashed the full force of their combined will. A blinding light erupted from their joined forms, engulfing the demonic entity.

The blinding light faded, leaving the chamber in an eerie stillness. As Blackwood's eyes adjusted, he saw Lord Percival Ashford, once the formidable Shadowmaster, now a broken figure slumped against the altar. The man's aristocratic features were twisted in disbelief; his carefully cultivated aura of power shattered like fine china.

Blackwood strode forward, his footsteps echoing in the cavernous space. "It's over, Ashford," he declared, his voice carrying the weight of hard-won victory. "Your reign of terror ends here."

Ashford's eyes, once gleaming with malevolent ambition, now darted about like those of a cornered animal. "You don't understand," he stammered, his usual eloquence deserting him.

"The power... it was meant to bring order, to elevate humanity!"

"Order?" Blackwood scoffed, his piercing blue eyes narrowing. "You speak of order when countless innocents have suffered at your hands?" He leaned in, his voice dropping to a dangerous whisper. "Tell me, Ashford, how many lives were sacrificed for your twisted vision?"

As Ashford fumbled for words, Blackwood's mind raced. "How deep does this corruption run?" he wondered. "How many others were complicit in these dark machinations?"

Lady Eleanor Ravenscroft materialized beside him, her ethereal form casting a soft glow. "Well done, Arthur," she murmured, her voice carrying centuries of sorrow and newfound hope. "At last, justice may be served."

Blackwood nodded, a mix of gratitude and awe washing over him. "We couldn't have done this without you, Lady Ravenscroft," he said softly. Your guidance and strength were invaluable."

The spectral noblewoman's form seemed to flicker, a peaceful smile gracing her translucent features. "Our journey together has come to its end, Detective," she said, her voice growing fainter. "My spirit can finally rest, knowing the truth has been unveiled."

As Lady Ravenscroft's form began to fade, Blackwood felt a pang of loss mingled with profound respect. He turned back to Ashford, and his resolve strengthened. "Now," he said, his voice steely, "you will answer for every life ruined, every dark deed committed in the name of your Order. The truth will come to light, Ashford, and justice will be served."

Blackwood's piercing blue eyes swept across the chamber, taking in the remnants of the supernatural battle. The once-glowing arcane symbols now lay dormant on the cold stone floor, their sinister power extinguished. He inhaled deeply, the air no longer heavy with malevolence but tinged with the acrid scent of spent energy.

"It's over," he muttered, more to himself than to the subdued Ashford. "But at what cost?"

His gaze fell upon Lord Percival Ashford's cowering form, the man's aristocratic features now twisted with fear and desperation.

Blackwood approached him, his footsteps echoing in the cavernous space.

"You'll be coming with me, Ashford," Blackwood declared, his voice firm yet tinged with weariness. "There's a reckoning to be had, not just for you."

Ashford looked up, a flicker of his former arrogance briefly crossing his face. "You fool," he spat. "Do you truly believe it ends here? The Order's reach extends far beyond these walls."

Blackwood's jaw tightened, his mind racing with the implications. He had dismantled the heart of the Order's power, but how many tendrils of corruption still writhed in the shadows of London's fogbound streets?

"Then we'll root out every last one," Blackwood replied, his determination evident in the set of his shoulders. "Your confederates, your benefactors—all will be brought to light."

As he secured Ashford with a pair of iron manacles, Blackwood's thoughts turned to the arduous path ahead. The battle within these walls had been won, but he knew the war against the darkness infesting London was far from over.

"Come," he said, guiding the defeated Ashford towards the chamber's exit. "There's a fog-shrouded city out there, teeming with secrets. And I intend to uncover them all, no matter the cost."

Chapter 17: Resolution

The acrid stench of sulfur hung in the air as Detective Arthur Blackwood surveyed the remnants of the Order's sanctum. Shattered glass crunched beneath his boots, and overturned furniture cast long shadows in the flickering candlelight. Where an oppressive darkness had once reigned, now only emptiness remained.

Blackwood's piercing blue eyes scanned the room, taking in every detail. His mind raced, piecing together the confrontation that had unfolded mere moments ago. The hair on the back of his neck still stood on end, a lingering reminder of the supernatural forces that had clashed within these walls.

"It's over," he murmured to himself, his voice barely above a whisper. "The menace that haunted this place is gone."

As if on cue, a muffled groan emanated from a darkened corner. Blackwood turned sharply, his hand instinctively moving to the revolver at his hip. From the shadows emerged a figure in tattered robes, stumbling and disoriented.

"Stay where you are," Blackwood commanded, his tone carrying an unmistakable authority.

The robed figure froze, swaying slightly. "What... what has happened?" the man asked, his voice trembling.

Blackwood approached cautiously, noting the confusion in the man's eyes. "Your Order has been dismantled," he stated firmly. "The dark influence you wielded is no more."

As he spoke, more figures emerged from various hiding places, each bearing the same look of bewilderment. Blackwood's keen intuition told him these were not the true architects of the Order's malevolence but its misguided followers.

"Constable!" Blackwood called out, his voice echoing through the cavernous room. "Bring in your men. We have some lost souls here in need of guidance... and incarceration."

As the police officers filed in, Blackwood contemplated the fragile nature of human will. How easily these people had been swayed by promises of power and enlightenment, only to find themselves pawns in a game beyond their comprehension.

One of the robed figures, a woman with haunted eyes, approached Blackwood. "Detective," she whispered, "what will become of us?"

Blackwood regarded her with a mixture of pity and resolve. "Justice will be served," he replied, "but perhaps in time, redemption may also be possible. Your dark path has ended, but a new one lies before you."

As the last of the Order's members were led away in shackles, Blackwood felt a weight lift from his shoulders. Yet, he knew this victory was one battle in an ongoing war against the unseen forces that threatened the very fabric of society.

"The Order is finished," he mused inwardly, "but how many other secrets lurk in the shadows of our fair city? How many more lost souls will be tempted by the promise of forbidden knowledge?"

With a deep sigh, Blackwood straightened his coat and prepared to face the fog-shrouded streets of London once more. The night was far from over, and he knew his work had only begun in this city of endless mysteries.

As Blackwood turned to leave the sanctum, a chill whispered through the air. The flickering gaslight cast his shadow long against the wall, and in its wavering edges, another form materialized. Lady Eleanor Ravenscroft appeared beside him, her ethereal presence more serene than he had ever witnessed.

"Detective Blackwood," she spoke, her voice an otherworldly echo that seemed to emanate from the stones around them. "The time has come for truths long buried to see the light of day."

Blackwood's piercing blue eyes met her translucent gaze. "Lady Ravenscroft, I'm listening."

She raised a delicate, spectral hand, gesturing to the air around them. As she did so, the sanctum seemed to shimmer and fade, replaced by visions of a grand ballroom from centuries past.

"It was here," Lady Ravenscroft began, her form now adorned in the opulent finery of her mortal days, "that my fate was sealed."

Blackwood found himself transported, a silent observer of the unfolding scene. He watched as a younger Lady Ravenscroft, resplendent in silk and jewels, moved gracefully through a sea of masked revelers.

"I was foolish," her voice continued, tinged with regret. "Blinded by ambition and the promise of power beyond mortal ken."

The Detective's brow furrowed. "The Order," he murmured, pieces falling into place within his mind.

Lady Ravenscroft nodded, her spectral form flickering between past and present. "They approached me that night, whispering of ancient secrets and forbidden knowledge. I, in my arrogance, believed I could master such forces."

The vision shifted, and Blackwood witnessed clandestine meetings in shadowed alcoves, arcane rituals performed by candlelight. He saw Lady Ravenscroft's eager participation, her growing obsession with the Order's dark promises.

"But at what cost, my lady?" Blackwood asked, his voice low and filled with empathy.

The ghost's eyes shimmered with ethereal tears.

"Everything, Detective. My life, my soul, my very essence. The Order's true aims were far more sinister than I imagined."

As she spoke, the visions around them grew darker, more chaotic. Blackwood watched in horror as the young Lady Ravenscroft realized her error too late, her desperate attempts to escape the Order's clutches ending in tragedy.

"They bound me to this realm," Lady Ravenscroft concluded, her form again translucent and ghostly. "A fate worse than death, to witness centuries of their machinations without the power to intervene."

Blackwood's mind raced, connecting the threads of this centuries-old mystery to the present. "And now, with the Order's fall, you can finally find peace?"

A sad smile graced Lady Ravenscroft's spectral features. "Perhaps, Detective. But first, there are truths you must know, secrets that have long festered in the shadows of our fair city."

As the visions faded and the sanctum's gloomy reality reasserted, Blackwood steeled himself for the revelations to come. The weight of history and the whispers of the supernatural pressed upon him, reminding him once again of the fine line he walked between the world of the living and the realms beyond.

Blackwood's piercing blue eyes fixed upon Lady Ravenscroft's fading form, his brow furrowed with a mixture of empathy and resolute determination. The sanctum's air hung heavy with the remnants of supernatural energy, a palpable reminder of the confrontation that had just transpired.

"My lady," Blackwood spoke, his voice low and measured, "your tale is one of great sorrow and injustice. As a law servant and man who has glimpsed the mysteries that lie beyond our mortal understanding, I give you my word that I shall see justice done. Your memory will not fade into obscurity, nor will the Order's crimes go unpunished."

Lady Ravenscroft's ethereal form brightened momentarily at his words. "Thank you, Detective. Your compassion brings me solace in these final moments."

As her spirit began to dissipate, the click of determined footsteps echoed through the chamber. Blackwood turned to see Evelyn Bradshaw approaching, her eyes wide with a mixture of relief and curiosity. Her typically impeccable attire was slightly disheveled, a testament to the night's harrowing events.

"Detective Blackwood," Evelyn called out, her voice steady despite the tremor in her hands. "Is it truly over? The Order..."

Blackwood nodded solemnly. "Indeed, Miss Bradshaw. The Order's reign of terror has come to an end."

Evelyn's shoulders sagged with visible relief. "I can scarcely believe it. Your courage and resolve in the face of such otherworldly horrors... I must express my deepest gratitude."

"Your own bravery played no small part in this outcome," Blackwood replied, his mind racing with the implications of their victory. "Tell me, what became of the remaining members?"

The fog-laden air hung heavy in the sanctum as Blackwood and Evelyn stood amidst the remnants of the Order's lair. The flickering gas lamps struggled to penetrate the gloom, casting shadows on the walls.

"The authorities have taken the surviving members into custody," Evelyn replied, her keen eyes scanning the room. "But I fear this is only the beginning of a greater unraveling."

Blackwood nodded, his piercing blue gaze fixed on the far wall. "Indeed, Miss Bradshaw. The Order's tendrils run deep through London's underbelly. Their absence will create a void that less savory elements will rush to fill."

Evelyn stepped closer, her voice lowered. "Do you believe we've truly seen the last of their influence?"

"I've learned that in our line of work, certainty is a luxury we can ill afford," Blackwood mused, running a hand through his tousled hair. "But we've dealt them a crippling blow. The bonds we've forged in this crucible will serve us well in the battles to come."

A wry smile played on Evelyn's lips. "Bonds forged in supernatural fire, no less. Detective, I must confess that this ordeal has shaken my skepticism to its core."

Blackwood's expression softened, a rare vulnerability crossing his features. "As it has mine, Miss Bradshaw. As it has mine."

He turned away, his thoughts churning like the fog outside. The weight of the investigation pressed upon him, memories of spectral encounters and eldritch horrors flashing unbidden through his mind.

"Arthur?" Evelyn's voice cut through his reverie, concern evident in her tone.

Blackwood blinked, realizing he had been lost in thought. "Forgive me. I find myself... altered by what we've witnessed. The veil between worlds has been lifted, if only for a moment, and I fear I shall never view our city in quite the same light again."

Evelyn placed a gentle hand on his arm. "None of us will, I suspect. But perhaps that's not entirely a curse. We've gained insight few others possess."

Blackwood nodded, his voice barely above a whisper. "At what cost, I wonder? The things I've seen... they haunt me, Evelyn. The spectral manifestations, the arcane rituals... how does one reconcile such experiences with the rational world we once knew?"

Blackwood's piercing blue eyes scanned the dimly lit sanctum, his resolve hardening with each passing moment. The air hung heavy with the remnants of supernatural energy, a tangible reminder of the unseen forces that had shaped their harrowing journey.

"We stand at a crossroads, Miss Bradshaw," he said, his voice low and measured. "The Order may be dismantled, but the veil between worlds remains thin. Our work... my work... is far from over."

Evelyn tilted her head, curiosity gleaming in her eyes. "You mean to continue investigating the supernatural, then?"

Blackwood nodded, a wry smile tugging at the corner of his lips. "I find myself uniquely positioned now. To turn away from these truths would be a disservice to both the living and the dead."

He paused, running a hand through his tousled dark hair. "But I must tread carefully. Skepticism remains vital, even as I open myself to possibilities beyond mortal ken."

As if summoned by his words, a shimmering apparition materialized before them. Lady Eleanor Ravenscroft's ethereal form coalesced, her delicate features etched with an expression of profound relief.

"Detective Blackwood," she intoned, her voice carrying the echo of centuries past. "I cannot express the depth of my gratitude. Through your courage and persistence, I finally found the answers I sought."

Blackwood bowed his head slightly, a gesture of respect. "Your own strength guided us, my lady. I merely followed the path you illuminated."

Lady Ravenscroft's spectral form began to flicker, her edges growing indistinct. "You have given me peace, Arthur Blackwood. May you find your own knowing that justice has been served."

As her spirit began to dissipate, Blackwood felt a curious mixture of fulfillment and melancholy wash over him. "Farewell, Lady Ravenscroft," he murmured. "May you find rest in realms beyond our understanding."

The last wisps of her presence faded, leaving behind a sense of completion that settled deep in Blackwood's bones. He turned to Evelyn, his expression one of quiet determination.

"And so," he said softly, "we step forward into a world forever changed, yet in need of guardians more than ever."

Blackwood's gaze lingered on the space where Lady Ravenscroft had been, his mind grappling with the profound implications of what he'd witnessed. Once impenetrable to his rational mind, the veil between worlds now seemed gossamer-thin.

"It's a peculiar thing, Miss Bradshaw," he mused, his voice low and contemplative. "To stand at the precipice of two realms, knowing that our actions here ripple through both."

Evelyn stepped closer, her keen eyes searching for Blackwood's face. "And how does that knowledge sit with you, Detective?" she inquired, her tone a mixture of curiosity and concern.

Blackwood's lips curved into a wry smile. "It's a weighty responsibility, to be sure. But one I find myself eager to shoulder."

Blackwood moved towards the sanctum's exit as they spoke, his steps measured and purposeful. Evelyn fell in beside him, matching his stride.

"The fog thickens," Blackwood observed as they stepped onto the cobblestones. The familiar streets of London were transformed into a ghostly labyrinth, gas lamps struggling to pierce the gloom.

Evelyn pulled her coat tighter around her.

"Much like the mysteries we've yet to unravel, I'd wager."

Blackwood chuckled, a rare sound from the usually somber Detective. "Indeed. Though I dare say we're better equipped to navigate both now."

As they walked, their footsteps muffled by the dense air, Blackwood's mind raced with possibilities. The Order's fall had left a void in London's underworld, one that mundane and otherworldly new threats would undoubtedly fill.

"I suspect our work is far from over, Miss Bradshaw," he said, his tone tinged with anticipation rather than dread.

Evelyn's eyes sparkled with determination. "I should hope not, Detective. There are still countless stories waiting to be uncovered, truths to be brought to light."

Blackwood nodded, feeling a surge of gratitude for his companion's unwavering spirit.

"Then let us be the ones to shine that light, however feeble it may seem against the darkness."

Blackwood felt a renewed sense of purpose coursing through him as they ventured deeper into the fog-shrouded streets. The path ahead was uncertain, fraught with danger and the unknown, but he was ready to face it head-on, with Evelyn by his side and the lessons of the past to guide him.

Blackwood paused at the corner, his keen eyes drawn back to the looming silhouette of the sanctum. The once-foreboding structure now stood silent, its windows dark and lifeless. A shiver ran down his spine, not from fear but from the weight of all that had transpired within those walls.

"Arthur?" Evelyn's voice cut through his reverie. "Is everything alright?"

He turned to her, his piercing blue eyes softening slightly. "Just... contemplating, Miss Bradshaw. It's a peculiar feeling. To stand on the precipice of a new chapter, knowing all we've left behind."

Evelyn nodded her gaze, following him to the sanctum. "It's as if the very air has changed. The fog seems less... oppressive somehow."

Blackwood's hand unconsciously moved to his coat pocket, fingering the small notebook that held their uncovered secrets. "We've struck a blow against the darkness, to be sure. But I can't help but wonder what other shadows lurk in London's corners, waiting to be brought to light."

As he spoke, Blackwood felt a familiar stirring in his chest—a mixture of trepidation and excitement that had driven him throughout his career. The sanctum may have fallen, but the city's mysteries remained endless, each one a siren call to his inquisitive mind.

"Well then, Detective," Evelyn said with a hint of a smile, "shall we seek out those shadows?"

Blackwood finally turned away from the sanctum, his shoulders set with quiet determination. "Indeed, we shall, Miss Bradshaw. Indeed, we shall." He offered her his arm, and together, they strode into the mist-shrouded street, ready to face whatever challenges lay ahead with newfound clarity and strength.

Chapter 18: Returning Home

The door creaked open, a sound that once seemed mundane but now carried an ominous weight. Detective Arthur Blackwood stepped onto the cobblestones, his boots echoing in the early morning stillness. The sun had barely crested the horizon, casting long shadows that stretched like grasping fingers across the street.

Blackwood paused, his piercing blue eyes scanning the familiar surroundings. The world looked different now, as if a veil had been lifted to reveal hidden depths. He straightened his coat, squaring his shoulders against an unseen burden.

"Another day begins," he murmured to himself, "but what secrets will it reveal?"

As he descended the street, the city began to awaken around him. Vendors called out their wares, their voices carrying a cheerfulness that felt discordant to Blackwood's mood. A horse-drawn carriage clattered past, the driver tipping his hat in greeting.

Blackwood nodded in return, his mind drifting.

The cacophony of London life seemed almost jarring after the otherworldly silence he'd recently experienced. He found himself hyper-aware of every sound and every movement as if expecting shadows to coalesce into spectral forms at any moment.

A street sweeper approached, his broom scraping against the cobblestones. "Mornin', sir," he said, touching his cap. "Looks to be a fine day."

"Indeed," Blackwood replied, his voice measured. "Though appearances can be deceiving, can they not?"

The sweeper gave him an odd look before continuing on his way. Blackwood sighed inwardly. How could he explain the weight of knowledge that now pressed upon him? The veil between worlds seemed thinner now, more permeable.

As he walked, Blackwood's thoughts turned inward. What other mysteries lay hidden beneath London's bustling exterior? How many more souls might be in peril from forces beyond mortal ken? His resolve strengthened with each step. He had been given a rare glimpse into the unknown and, with it, a duty to protect those who remained blissfully unaware.

The morning fog began to lift, revealing the city in all its Victorian splendor. Yet to Blackwood's eyes, shadows lingered where none should be, hinting at realms unseen. He squared his shoulders, ready to face whatever the day might bring. For in this city of secrets and spectral dangers, he stood as a guardian on the threshold between two worlds.

Arthur Blackwood's keen eyes caught sight of a young newspaper boy on the corner, his shrill voice piercing through the morning bustle.

"Extra! Extra! Read all about it! Mysterious disappearances in Whitechapel!"

A familiar tightness gripped Blackwood's chest as he approached the lad, fishing a coin from his pocket. "One paper, if you please," he said, his voice low and measured.

The boy's grimy hands thrust the freshly printed broadsheet into Blackwood's grasp. "There you are, guv'nor. Grim business, that."

Blackwood nodded absently, his piercing blue eyes already scanning the front page. He searched for any hint, any coded message that might reveal the Order's downfall to those who knew where to look. But there was nothing—only the mundane reports of petty crimes and society gossip.

"Hardly the whole story, is it?" Blackwood murmured to himself, folding the paper with a sigh. How many Londoners walked these streets, oblivious to the supernatural battles waged in the shadows? The weight of his recent experiences pressed heavily upon him.

As he continued his walk, a familiar figure emerged from the thinning fog. Agnes O'Reilly, his landlady, stood before her modest boarding house, a knowing smile playing at the corners of her lips.

"Good morning, Mr. Blackwood," she called, her voice warm and tinged with concern. "I trust you slept well?"

Blackwood doffed his hat. "As well as can be expected, Mrs. O'Reilly. Your concern is appreciated."

Agnes's eyes twinkled with unspoken understanding. "I've seen that look before, love.

The look of a man who's gazed into the abyss and lived to tell the tale."

Blackwood felt a rush of gratitude for the perceptive woman. "You've always had a knack for reading people, Mrs. O'Reilly. I daresay there's more to you than meets the eye."

She chuckled softly. "I've seen my share of oddities in this old city. But something tells me your recent adventures put mine to shame."

For a moment, Blackwood considered unburdening himself, sharing the horrors and wonders he'd witnessed. But he held back, unwilling to draw Agnes into the dangerous world he now inhabited.

"Let's just say," he replied carefully, "that London holds more secrets than I ever imagined. And I intend to uncover them all."

Agnes nodded her expression, a mixture of pride and concern. "Just remember, Mr. Blackwood, that even the bravest souls need a safe harbor now and then. My door is always open to you."

As Blackwood tipped his hat in farewell, he felt a warmth in his chest, a reminder that human kindness could still shine through the gloom, even in the face of cosmic horrors.

The imposing stone facade of Scotland Yard loomed before Detective Arthur Blackwood, its windows glinting like watchful eyes in the pale morning light. As he ascended the steps, the familiar weight of responsibility settled upon his shoulders, heavier now with the knowledge of unseen forces that lurked beyond the veil of ordinary perception.

Constable Finch greeted him at the entrance, his ruddy face creased with a mixture of admiration and trepidation. "Welcome back, Detective Blackwood. Quite the talk about town, your latest case."

Blackwood met the young officer's gaze, his voice measured and low. "Is that so, Finch? And what, pray tell, are they saying?"

"Oh, bits and bobs, sir. Whispers of occult doings and ghostly apparitions. But you know how people love to embellish."

A wry smile tugged at Blackwood's lips. "Indeed, they do. Best we focus on the facts, wouldn't you agree?"

As he made his way through the bustling corridors, Blackwood found himself the subject of furtive glances and hushed conversations.

He nodded curtly to his colleagues, careful to maintain an air of professional detachment.

Inspector Graves intercepted him near the records room, his bushy eyebrows knitted with concern. "Blackwood, a word if you please."

"Certainly, Inspector," Blackwood replied, following the older man into a quiet alcove.

Graves leaned in his voice barely above a whisper. "There's talk of... unusual circumstances surrounding your last case. The higher-ups are asking questions."

Blackwood's mind raced, weighing the consequences of full disclosure against the need for discretion. "The case was... complex, sir. But I assure you, every action taken was in service of justice and the protection of the public."

"And the reports of... supernatural occurrences?"

A chill ran down Blackwood's spine as he recalled the ethereal glow of Lady Ravenscroft's spectral form. "Merely the product of overactive imaginations and tricks of the light, I'm sure. You know how witnesses can be in times of stress."

Graves studied him for a long moment before nodding. "Very well, Blackwood. I trust your judgment. But tread carefully. There are some truths the world may not be ready to face."

As Blackwood finally reached the sanctuary of his office, he allowed himself a moment of quiet reflection. The case files strewn across his desk seemed to whisper of hidden dangers and unexplored mysteries. He ran his fingers along the edge of a particularly worn folder, his mind churning with possibilities.

"What secrets do you hold?" he murmured, a newfound sense of purpose kindling within him.

"What truths lie buried beneath the veneer of our mundane existence?"

With a deep breath, Blackwood settled into his chair, ready to delve once more into the shadowy underbelly of London. The world, he now knew, was far stranger and more perilous than he had ever imagined. And he, Arthur Blackwood, stood as a sentinel against the encroaching darkness, armed with nothing but his wits, his courage, and the hard-won knowledge that some battles must be fought in silence, beyond the ken of ordinary men.

The clatter of typewriter keys filled the air of the bustling newsroom, a cacophony broken only by the occasional shout of an editor or the rustling of papers. Amidst this controlled chaos, Evelyn Bradshaw's fingers danced across her typewriter with practiced precision, her brow furrowed in concentration as she crafted her latest exposé.

"...and so, dear readers, we must ask ourselves: what other secrets lurk beneath the cobblestone streets of our fair city?" Evelyn muttered, her voice barely audible above the din. She paused, green eyes scanning the words before her with a critical gaze.

A nearby colleague called out, "Got another scoop for us, Bradshaw?"

Evelyn's lips curved into a cryptic smile. "Oh, you have no idea, Thomas. This city's underbelly is writhing with stories just waiting to be told."

As she turned back to her work, her gaze flickered to the bulletin board beside her desk.

Among press clippings and scribbled notes was a photograph of Detective Arthur Blackwood.

His piercing blue eyes seemed to stare back at her, a reminder of their shared harrowing adventure.

"Penny, for your thoughts?" asked Sarah, a junior reporter, noticing Evelyn's distraction.

Evelyn chuckled softly. "I was just thinking about how life has a way of thrusting the most unlikely allies into our path." Her fingers absently traced the edge of Blackwood's photograph.

"Sometimes, Sarah, truth is a burden we must shoulder together, lest it crush us under its weight."

"Sounds like there's quite a story there," Sarah prodded gently.

Evelyn's eyes sparkled with a mix of mischief and determination. "Oh, there is. But some tales are best left untold... for now." She turned back to her typewriter, her voice dropping to a whisper. "After all, my dear Blackwood, our work has only just begun."

The heavy doors of Scotland Yard creaked shut behind Detective Arthur Blackwood as he stepped out into the waning afternoon light.

London's usual frenetic pace seemed muted, and the city was bathed in an amber glow that softened its harsh edges. Blackwood paused, his keen eyes scanning the bustling street before him, a subtle furrow creasing his brow.

"Blasted paperwork," he muttered under his breath, rolling his shoulders to ease the tension.

"A cup of tea is what's needed now."

With purposeful strides, Blackwood set off towards Mulligan's, a quaint café nestled between a bookshop and a tobacconist. The familiar jingle of the bell above the door greeted him as he entered, the aroma of freshly baked scones and Earl Grey enveloping him like a comforting embrace.

"Well, if it isn't the good detective!" boomed Mr. Mulligan from behind the counter, his ruddy face creased with a broad smile. "The usual, I presume?"

Blackwood nodded, settling into his favored corner table. "If you'd be so kind, Mulligan. It's been a rather... taxing day."

As the proprietor busied himself with the tea, Blackwood's thoughts drifted. The café's warm ambiance faded, replaced by the haunting image of Lady Ravenscroft's ethereal form. Her words echoed in his mind, a spectral whisper that sent a shiver down his spine.

"Your tea, sir," Mulligan's voice cut through Blackwood's reverie. "If you don't mind my saying, you look like you've seen a ghost."

A wry smile played at the corners of Blackwood's mouth. "Perhaps I have, old friend. Perhaps I have."

Blackwood lifted the delicate porcelain cup to his lips, the warmth of the tea seeping into his hands. His piercing blue eyes gazed unseeing at the bustling street beyond the café window as he sipped. The mundane scene before him seemed to flicker, like a veil threatening to part, revealing glimpses of a world unseen by most.

"The line between our world and the next," he mused aloud, his voice barely above a whisper, "it's far thinner than I ever imagined."

A young woman at a nearby table glanced at him curiously, but Blackwood paid her no mind.

His thoughts raced, recalling the otherworldly encounters that had shaken the very foundations of his reality.

"Everything I've witnessed," he continued, speaking more to himself than anyone else, "it changes a man. How does one go back to ordinary life after glimpsing the extraordinary?"

Draining the last of his tea, Blackwood rose, nodding his thanks to Mulligan. As he stepped out into the afternoon light, the cobblestones beneath his feet felt solid, reassuringly real. His path led him to a nearby park, where the laughter of children playing cut through the fog of his ruminations.

A small boy chasing a hoop tumbled at Blackwood's feet. The Detective helped him up with a gentle hand.

"There you are, lad. No harm done, I trust?"

The child beamed up at him. "No, sir! Thank you!"

As the boy scampered off, Blackwood felt a tightness in his chest, at ease. "This," he thought, watching the carefree games unfold before him, "this innocence is what I'm sworn to protect—from threats both seen and unseen."

The familiar creak of the stairs to his lodgings echoed in the dimming light of dusk, each step a comforting rhythm that anchored Blackwood to the present. He paused at the landing, resting his hand on the worn banister, and drew a deep breath. The scent of Mrs. O'Reilly's cooking wafted up from below, a homely aroma that seemed to chase away the lingering shadows of his thoughts.

Blackwood's gaze swept over the familiar surroundings as he entered his room. The gas lamp on his desk flickered to life with a soft hiss, casting a warm glow over the cluttered surface. He sank into his chair, the leather creaking beneath him, and allowed himself a moment of quiet reflection.

"What a day," he murmured, rubbing his temples. "To think, just this morning, I walked these streets a changed man, and now..."

His eyes fell upon a blank sheet of paper, and with a sudden surge of purpose, he reached for his pen. The nib scratched softly against the paper as he began to write.

"My dear Miss Bradshaw," he read aloud as he wrote, his voice low and measured. "I am compelled to put pen to paper to express my deepest gratitude for your unwavering support and courage during our recent... escapade."

Blackwood paused, a wry smile tugging at his lips. "Escapade," he mused. "As if we'd merely taken a stroll through Hyde Park rather than..."

He shook his head, returning to his letter. "Your quick wit and fearless determination were invaluable in navigating the perilous waters we found ourselves in. I dare say, without your presence, the outcome might have been far less favorable."

As he wrote, Blackwood's mind wandered to their shared experiences and the dangers they had faced together. "I find myself contemplating the strength of our partnership," he continued, his pen moving swiftly across the page. It occurs to me that future collaborations may be on the horizon, should you be so inclined. The world, it seems, holds more mysteries than either of us initially suspected."

He leaned back in his chair, considering his following words carefully. "What do you say, Miss Bradshaw? Are you prepared to delve deeper into the shadows that lurk beneath London's foggy streets?"

Blackwood set down his pen and rose from the desk, letter complete. He crossed to the window, its panes streaked with the last vestiges of an earlier rain. As he gazed out, the cityscape of London unfurled before him, bathed in the soft glow of twilight.

Gas lamps flickered to life along the cobblestone streets, their warm light pushing back against the encroaching darkness. The ever-present fog began its nightly dance, weaving between buildings and blurring the lines between the mundane and the mysterious.

"What secrets do you hide tonight, old girl?"

Blackwood murmured, his breath fogging the glass.

He pressed his forehead against the cool window, allowing the chill to ground him in the present. His piercing blue eyes scanned the streets below, watching as shadowy figures hurried home, unaware of the unseen world that existed alongside their own.

"So many mysteries," he whispered, "so many truths yet to be uncovered."

A flicker of movement caught his attention—a cat darting across an alleyway, or perhaps something more sinister? Blackwood's hand instinctively moved to his pocket, where he kept a small vial of holy water, a habit born from too many encounters with the supernatural.

He chuckled softly at his own paranoia. "Steady on, old boy. Not every shadow hides a specter."

Yet as he continued to observe the city, Blackwood couldn't shake the feeling that London herself was alive, pulsing with secrets waiting to be discovered. His recent experiences had sharpened his senses, attuning him to the whispers of the hidden world.

"I'm not alone in this," he reminded himself, thinking of Evelyn Bradshaw and their burgeoning partnership. A warmth spread through his chest, dispelling some of the chills that had settled in his bones.

Blackwood straightened, squaring his shoulders as he faced his reflection in the glass. The man who stared back at him was changed—older, perhaps, but also wiser and more resolute.

"Whatever lies ahead," he said to his reflection, his voice low but firm, "we'll face it together. The truth will come out, no matter how deep it's buried."

As night fully embraced the city, Blackwood turned from the window, and his resolve strengthened. The quest for truth beckoned, and he was ready to answer its call.

Chapter 19: Reflection

The oil lamp's flame flickered, casting long shadows across the weathered oak table.

Detective Arthur Blackwood gazed into the depths of his teacup, his piercing blue eyes distant with remembrance. The silence in Agnes's cozy parlor hung thick as London fog, broken only by the soft ticking of the mantel clock.

Blackwood cleared his throat. "I... I must express my profound gratitude," he began, his voice low and measured. "Your companionship and unwavering support throughout this harrowing investigation have been..." He paused, searching for the right words. "Well, quite simply, invaluable."

Agnes's kind eyes crinkled with a warm smile while Evelyn leaned forward, her sharp gaze fixed on the Detective. Blackwood felt a tightness in his chest, recalling the dangers they had faced together.

"We've seen things that defy explanation," Evelyn mused, settling back in her chair. Her fingers drummed a restless rhythm on the armrest. "If you had told me a month ago that I'd be chasing specters through fogbound alleys, I'd have thought you mad." She shook her head, a wry smile playing on her lips.

Blackwood nodded solemnly. "The veil between worlds is thinner than most dare imagine."

Evelyn's eyes sparkled with newfound understanding. "It's as if I've been given a glimpse behind the curtain of reality itself. As a journalist, I've always prided myself on uncovering hidden truths, but this..." She gestured vaguely, searching for words. "This changes everything."

"How so, my dear?" Agnes inquired gently.

Evelyn's brow furrowed in contemplation. "I can no longer view the world through the same lens.

Every shadow now holds the potential for something... other. It's both terrifying and exhilarating."

Blackwood felt a pang of empathy. He remembered all too well the moment his own perception had irrevocably shifted. "The burden of such knowledge is not easily borne," he said softly, more to himself than to his companions.

The Detective's mind drifted to the fog-shrouded streets beyond the parlor's walls. In the eerie veil that cloaked London, how many unsuspecting souls walked past doorways to other realms, blissfully unaware of the thin membrane separating their world from the next?

Agnes leaned forward, her weathered hands clasping her teacup. The lamplight caught the silver in her hair, casting a soft halo around her face. "You know," she began, her voice warm and rich with memory, "your tale reminds me of so many I've heard within these very walls." Her eyes twinkled as she gazed at Blackwood and Evelyn. "My tenants, they come and go like leaves in the wind, each carrying their own burdens and secrets."

Blackwood's piercing blue eyes fixed on Agnes, his curiosity piqued. "What sort of tales, Mrs. O'Reilly?"

Agnes smiled, the corners of her eyes crinkling.

"Oh, stories of love and loss, of triumph over darkness. But the ones that stick with me most are those of redemption, my dears. The human spirit's capacity to rise above its own failings... it's truly remarkable."

Blackwood felt a tightness in his chest, his own past mistakes rising unbidden in his mind. He shifted in his chair, his gaze drifting to the window where tendrils of fog crept past like ghostly fingers.

"I've seen broken men and women walk through that door," Agnes continued, gesturing to the parlor entrance, "and leave transformed. It's not always grand or dramatic, mind you. Sometimes, it's as simple as finding the strength to face another day."

The Detective's thoughts churned, images of the horrors they'd faced flashing before his mind's eye. He spoke, his voice low and contemplative. "The truths we've uncovered... they weigh heavily. To know what lurks in the shadows, to understand the forces that shape our world..." He trailed off, searching for words.

"It changes a person," Agnes finished gently.

Blackwood nodded, meeting her understanding gaze. "Indeed it does, Mrs. O'Reilly. There's a responsibility that comes with such knowledge. A duty to..." He paused, his brow furrowing. "To what? Protect? Enlighten? Or perhaps to stand guard at the threshold between worlds?"

The room fell silent, save for the soft ticking of the clock on the mantelpiece. Blackwood's words hung in the air, heavy with implication.

He felt the weight of his role more acutely than ever before, a sentinel against the encroaching darkness that most would never see or comprehend.

Evelyn's soft yet resolute voice broke the contemplative silence. "We've paid a heavy price for our pursuit of justice," she said, her piercing eyes reflecting the flickering lamplight. Lives forever altered, innocence shattered..."

Her gaze fell to her hands, delicately cradling her teacup. "I can't help but think of young Thomas, the scullery boy at Lord Ashworth's estate. His wide-eyed terror when we discovered him in that hidden chamber, surrounded by arcane symbols..." Evelyn's voice caught a rare vulnerability from the usually composed journalist.

"Or Mrs. Hawkins," she continued, her tone tinged with regret. "A respectable widow, now committed to Bedlam, her mind fractured by what she witnessed during the Order's ritual."

Blackwood leaned forward, his face etched with concern. "We couldn't have foreseen all the consequences, Miss Bradshaw. We did what was necessary."

Agnes reached out, gently patting Evelyn's hand. "My dear, your actions have brought more good than harm. I've seen it before—loss and pain can lead to unexpected blessings."

The older woman's eyes grew distant as if peering into the past. "I remember a young woman who came to stay here years ago. Sarah, her name was. She'd lost everything—her husband, her child, her home—all in one terrible night..."

As Agnes recounted Sarah's tale of tragedy and redemption, Evelyn found herself drawn in, her journalist's instincts piqued despite her melancholy. She marveled at Agnes's ability to weave hope from the threads of despair, a skill born of years tending to the wounded souls who passed through her doors.

Blackwood listened intently to Agnes's tale, his piercing blue eyes fixed on the flickering gas lamp. As she finished, he ran a hand through his tousled dark hair, his expression a mixture of admiration and introspection.

"Your words resonate deeply, Mrs. O'Reilly," he said, his voice low and measured. "They remind me of my missteps along this treacherous path."

He paused, gathering his thoughts. "There were moments, in the depths of our investigation, when doubt gnawed at me like a ravenous beast. I questioned every decision, every intuition that had led us into the Order's web."

Evelyn leaned forward, her gaze fixed on Blackwood. She had rarely seen him so vulnerable, so willing to expose the cracks in his carefully constructed facade.

"I remember standing in that abandoned chapel," Blackwood continued, his eyes distant.

"The air thick with incense and... something else. Something ancient and malevolent. I felt it clawing at my sanity, whispering that we were fools to challenge forces beyond our comprehension."

He shook his head, a wry smile playing at the corners of his mouth. "But then I thought of the innocent lives at stake in the Order's machinations. And I knew, despite my fears, that our cause was just."

Evelyn nodded, her own eyes glinting with renewed determination. "You're right, Arthur," she said, using his Christian name in a rare moment of intimacy. "What we've uncovered, the truths we've dragged into the light—they matter."

She stood abruptly, pacing the small room with barely contained energy. "Think of it—how many dark corners have we illuminated? How many lies have been exposed?"

Blackwood watched her, a mix of admiration and concern etched on his features. "Indeed, Miss Bradshaw. But at what cost to yourself?"

Evelyn turned to face them, and her chin lifted defiantly. "A cost I'm willing to pay. This is my calling, Arthur. To seek the truth, no matter how deeply it's buried or how fiercely it's guarded."

She clenched her fist, her voice rising with passion. "I'll continue my work, armed with all we've learned. The Order may be defeated, but there are other shadows to chase, other mysteries to unravel."

The fervor of their exchange gradually faded, leaving the small room enveloped in a profound silence. The ancient clock on Agnes's mantelpiece ticked steadily, its rhythmic sound accentuating the weight of unspoken thoughts.

Blackwood leaned back in his chair, his eyes distant, while Evelyn's gaze was fixed on the flickering flame of the oil lamp. Ever the quiet observer, Agnes sat with her hands folded in her lap, a serene expression on her weathered face.

The comfortable quiet stretched on, broken only by the occasional creak of the floorboards or the muffled sounds of London's fogbound streets beyond the window. Each seemed lost in their reflections, the gravity of their shared ordeal hanging palpably in the air.

Blackwood's mind wandered to the shadowy corners they had explored, the veil between worlds they had dared to lift. He shuddered imperceptibly, feeling the phantom chill of otherworldly encounters.

After what seemed an eternity, Agnes rose from her seat, her movements as graceful as a woman half her age. She reached for the teapot, her eyes twinkling with motherly affection.

"Now then, my dears," she said softly, her voice barely above a whisper, "let's have one last cup before the night grows too old."

As she poured the steaming liquid into their cups, her hands steady and sure, Agnes paused, her expression growing serious. "If I may offer a final word of advice," she began, her tone gentle yet firm, "cherish these bonds you've forged through such trials. They're rare and precious things."

Blackwood looked up, meeting her gaze. "Indeed, they are, Mrs. O'Reilly," he murmured, a hint of emotion coloring his usually composed voice.

Agnes nodded, continuing as she handed Evelyn her cup. "And remember, loves, the world isn't as simple as we'd like it to be. There are forces at work that are always seeking to upset the balance. We must remain vigilant, even in times of peace."

Evelyn accepted the cup, and her brow furrowed in thought. "You speak as if from experience, Agnes," she observed, curiosity evident in her tone.

The older woman's smile held a touch of mystery. "Let's just say I've seen my share of London's secrets over the years, Miss Bradshaw. This old house has sheltered many a soul with tales to tell."

Detective Arthur Blackwood cradled the warm teacup in his hands, his piercing blue eyes softening as he gazed at Agnes. The flickering lamplight cast dancing shadows across his face, accentuating the lines of weariness etched there by countless sleepless nights and harrowing encounters.

"Mrs. O'Reilly," he began, his voice low and measured, "I find myself at a loss for words to express my gratitude. Your unwavering support throughout this ordeal has been... invaluable."

Blackwood paused, swallowing hard as he wrestled with emotions, he rarely allowed himself to display. In his mind's eye, he saw flashes of the horrors they had faced together—the ghostly apparitions, the ancient rituals, the very fabric of reality torn asunder. Yet through it all, Agnes had been their anchor, her boarding house a sanctuary amidst the storm.

"You've given me more than just a safe haven," he continued, his gaze fixed on the swirling tea leaves in his cup. "You've lent me strength when my own faltered and courage to face the unknown. I... I am not accustomed to relying on others, but I am profoundly grateful for our friendship."

Evelyn leaned forward, her eyes bright with emotion. "I couldn't agree more, Arthur," she said, her voice carrying a warmth that belied her usual sharp wit. "When I set out to uncover this story, I never imagined finding such steadfast allies."

She raised her cup, a smile playing at the corners of her lips. "To unexpected friendships," Evelyn declared, her tone both solemn and joyous. "And to hard-won victories against forces that would plunge our world into darkness."

The clink of their cups meeting resonated in the cozy room, a sound that seemed to echo with the weight of all they had endured and overcome together.

As the final drops of tea were drained and the clock's gentle chime signaled the late hour, the trio rose from their seats, the floorboards creaking softly beneath their feet. Arthur Blackwood felt a sudden tightness in his chest, a reluctance to leave this haven of warmth and companionship.

"I suppose this is where we part ways," he said, his voice low and tinged with an uncharacteristic hint of emotion.

Agnes stepped forward, her weathered hands clasping his. "Not forever, my dear," she assured him, her eyes twinkling with maternal affection.

"My door is always open to you both."

Evelyn moved to join them, her journalistic composure momentarily slipping as she fiercely embraced Agnes. "Thank you," she whispered, her words muffled against the older woman's shoulder. "For everything."

Blackwood watched the exchange, a lump forming in his throat. He had always prided himself on his solitary nature, but now he understood the power of connection. As Evelyn turned to him, he found himself pulling her into an embrace, surprising them both.

"We've seen things that would shatter most minds," he murmured his usual stoicism cracking. "I'm glad I didn't face them alone."

Evelyn pulled back, her eyes glistening. "We'll stay in touch," she said firmly. "After all, who knows what other mysteries await us?"

With final handshakes and promises of future visits, Blackwood stepped out into the fog-laden streets of London. The gas lamps cast eerie halos in the mist, their light barely penetrating the gloom. He paused, drawing his coat tighter around him as he absorbed the stark contrast between the warmth he'd just left and the chill that now enveloped him.

As he began to walk, his footsteps echoing hollowly on the cobblestones, Blackwood's mind whirled with the revelations of their shared ordeal. The veil between worlds, once so impenetrable to his rational mind, now seemed gossamer-thin. Every shadow held the potential for mystery, every whisper of wind the possibility of otherworldly communication.

"I've been changed," he thought, his pace steady despite the uneven ground. "We've all been changed. And yet..."

He paused, glancing back at the faint glow of Agnes's boarding house windows. A small smile tugged at his lips.

"And yet, we're stronger for it. More prepared for whatever darkness may come."

Detective Arthur Blackwood strode into the foggy night with renewed purpose, ready to face whatever unseen forces might threaten the delicate balance between the worlds he now knew existed.

Detective Arthur Blackwood paused, his silhouette a stark contrast against the swirling fog. He turned, his piercing blue eyes settling on the warm glow emanating from Agnes's boarding house windows. A faint smile played upon his lips, a rare expression for the usually stoic Detective.

"What lies ahead, I wonder?" he mused aloud, his measured voice barely above a whisper.

The gas lamps flickered, casting elongated shadows that danced across the cobblestones.

Blackwood's gaze swept the eerie thoroughfare, and his senses heightened to the whispers of the unseen world that now constantly brushed against his consciousness.

"The veil has been lifted," he thought, a shiver running down his spine that had nothing to do with the damp chill. "And with it, a burden of knowledge that cannot be unlearned."

He took a step forward, then hesitated, turning once more to look at the sanctuary he had just left. The boarding house stood as a beacon of warmth and companionship in the midst of London's ghostly shroud.

"I've walked these streets a thousand times," Blackwood said softly to himself, "and yet, they've never felt quite so... alive."

His hand instinctively moved to his coat pocket, fingers brushing against the notebook that held the cryptic clues of their recent adventure. The notebook's weight seemed to ground him, a tangible reminder of their uncovered truths.

"The world is full of mysteries," he mused, his voice gaining strength. "But so too is it full of those who would seek to solve them."

With a final nod towards the boarding house, Blackwood squared his shoulders and set off into the fog-laden night. His steps were purposeful, his resolve unwavering. The unseen eyes of London watched as he disappeared into the mist, a guardian of secrets and a seeker of truths, ready to face whatever enigmas the future might hold.

Chapter 20: Epilogue

Detective Arthur Blackwood stood motionless in the center of the dimly lit study, his keen eyes surveying the aftermath of the confrontation that had unfolded mere moments ago. The flickering gas lamps cast long shadows across the room, their feeble light barely penetrating the gloom that seemed to cling to every surface. He drew in a deep breath, tasting the lingering scent of sulfur and decay on his tongue.

"By God," he murmured, his voice barely above a whisper, "what manner of evil have we vanquished this night?"

A faint shimmer caught his eye as he spoke—a gossamer thread of ethereal light hovering near the far wall. Lady Eleanor Ravenscroft's spirit materialized in translucent form, a stark contrast to the room's oppressive darkness.

"We have triumphed, Detective Blackwood," she intoned, her voice carrying the echoes of centuries past. "Though at great cost."

Blackwood nodded solemnly, his piercing blue eyes meeting her otherworldly gaze. "Indeed, my lady. Your courage in the face of such malevolence was... remarkable."

He took a tentative step towards her, his mind racing to process the night's events. The weight of their shared ordeal pressed upon him, a reminder of the thin veil between the world of the living and that which lay beyond.

"I fear our journey together nears its end," Lady Ravenscroft said, a note of melancholy in her ethereal voice.

Blackwood felt a pang of regret, knowing that their unlikely partnership had reached its conclusion. "You have my eternal gratitude, Lady Eleanor. Without your guidance, I doubt we would have unraveled this infernal mystery."

As he spoke, Blackwood's gaze drifted to the shattered remnants of an ancient artifact lying on the floor - the very object that had bound

Lady Ravenscroft's spirit to this realm for centuries. Its destruction had been the key to their victory, yet he couldn't help but wonder at the cost.

"What becomes of you now?" he asked, his voice tinged with both curiosity and concern.

Lady Ravenscroft's form seemed to flicker as if buffeted by an unseen wind. "I go to face what lies beyond, Detective. My unfinished business in this world is at last complete."

Blackwood nodded a mixture of emotions washing over him. Relief at their success warred with a sense of loss at the impending departure of his spectral companion. He had grown accustomed to her presence, her centuries of wisdom proving invaluable in their investigation.

"Then I bid you farewell, my lady," he said, bowing his head slightly. "May you find the peace that eluded you for so long."

As Lady Ravenscroft's spirit began to fade, Blackwood couldn't help but reflect on the bizarre turn his life had taken. Once a man of pure logic and reason, he now stood as a bridge between two worlds, forever changed by the truths he had uncovered.

Lady Ravenscroft's ethereal form shimmered, her once-vibrant presence now fading like mist before the morning sun. Blackwood's piercing blue eyes fixed upon her, his brow furrowed with a mixture of awe and melancholy.

"I feel it, Detective," she whispered, her voice carrying an otherworldly echo. "The veil between worlds grows thin."

Blackwood took a step forward, his hand instinctively reaching out before falling back to his side. "You've shown remarkable courage, Lady Eleanor. Your determination to see justice done, even from beyond the grave, is... extraordinary."

A soft, sad smile played across Lady Ravenscroft's translucent features. "As have you, Arthur. You've given me the closure I've sought for centuries."

Blackwood felt a tightness in his chest as her form grew more diaphanous. He pondered the strange bonds forged in the crucible of this investigation - a partnership that transcended the boundaries of life and death.

"I shall carry the lessons of our journey with me always," he said, his usually measured voice thick with emotion.

Lady Ravenscroft's apparition began to dissolve, her once-regal form now a gossamer wisp. Her final words floated on the air like a fading sigh: "Remember, Detective, the veil is thin. We may yet meet again..."

Blackwood watched, transfixed, as her ethereal beauty melted into the ether. Her presence's last glimmer winked like a distant star, leaving him alone in the study's oppressive silence.

"Godspeed, Lady Eleanor," he whispered to the empty room, his words a quiet benediction.

"May you find the peace you so richly deserve."

Blackwood stood motionless, his piercing blue eyes fixed on the spot where Lady Ravenscroft had vanished. The weight of the case settled upon him like a heavy cloak, and he felt the familiar tug of introspection pulling at his thoughts.

"What a curious journey this has been," he mused aloud, his voice barely above a whisper.

"To think, the veil between worlds is far more permeable than I once believed."

He paced the study, fingers tracing the leather-bound spines of ancient tomes lining the shelves. Each step echoed with the gravity of newfound knowledge.

"And yet," Blackwood continued, his brow furrowing, "how many more secrets lie hidden in the shadows of our fair city? How many more restless spirits cry out for justice?"

The Detective paused by the window, gazing out at the fog-shrouded streets of London. His reflection stared back at him, a man changed by his supernatural encounters.

With a deep breath, Blackwood straightened his coat and made for the door. "No rest for the wicked," he muttered, "nor for those who hunt them."

As he stepped out into the chill night air, the fog curled around his ankles like a living thing. The familiar sounds of Victorian London—the distant clip-clop of hooves, the muffled voices of late-night revelers—seemed somehow muted, as if the city itself were holding its breath.

Blackwood set off down the cobblestone street, his footsteps purposeful. "I've peered behind the curtain now," he thought, pulling his collar up against the damp. "There's no going back to blissful ignorance. The unseen world is as real as the cobbles beneath my feet."

A flicker of movement caught his eye—perhaps a stray cat or something more ethereal? Blackwood quickened his pace, his mind awhirl with the implications of all he had witnessed.

As Blackwood rounded a corner, the gaslight cast long shadows that seemed to dance and writhe in the fog. He paused, his keen eyes scanning the murky alleyway before him.

"Curious," he murmured, his hand instinctively moving to the revolver concealed beneath his coat. "The veil between worlds grows thin in places like this."

A whisper, barely audible, drifted on the night air. Blackwood cocked his head, straining to discern words from the eerie sound.

"Who's there?" he called, his voice steady despite the chill that ran down his spine. "Show yourself!"

Only silence answered, but the Detective's intuition prickled. He took a cautious step forward, his eyes darting from shadow to shadow.

"Perhaps," Blackwood mused aloud, "it's not always about seeing. Sometimes, one must learn to listen with more than just the ears."

A gust of wind swept down the alley as if in response, carrying with it the faintest whisper of a woman's laughter. Blackwood spun, his coat flaring out behind him, but the street remained empty.

"Another mystery," he said, a wry smile tugging at his lips. "It seems Lady Ravenscroft's case was but the beginning."

The Detective continued on his way, his stride purposeful yet wary. Each shadowy doorway, each fog-shrouded corner seemed to promise new enigmas waiting to be unraveled.

"The game is afoot," Blackwood muttered to himself, echoing the words of his literary counterpart. "And I, for one, am eager to play."

Detective Arthur Blackwood paused before the weathered oak door of his lodgings, his keen eyes taking in the warm glow seeping through the gap beneath. A sigh of relief escaped his lips as he turned the key, the familiar creak of hinges welcoming him home.

"At last," he murmured, stepping into the modest foyer. The floorboards groaned softly beneath his feet, a sound as comforting as an old friend's greeting.

Blackwood shrugged off his coat, hanging it on the rack with practiced ease. His gaze fell upon the solitary lamp on the side table, its flame dancing merrily, casting long shadows across the room.

"How inviting you look tonight, old friend," he addressed the lamp with a weary smile. "You've no idea the sights I've seen."

As he moved further into the room, the Detective's eyes were drawn to a crisp white envelope resting on his writing desk. Curiosity piqued, he approached, his brow furrowing as he recognized the elegant script.

"What's this?" Blackwood muttered, reaching for the letter. "Surely not another summons so soon?"

With nimble fingers, he broke the seal and unfolded the paper within. His expression shifted from curiosity to intrigue as he scanned the contents.

"My word," he breathed, sinking into his chair. "It seems Lady Ravenscroft's case has opened more doors than it closed."

The letter spoke of whispers in high society, of secrets that could shake the very foundations of London's elite. Blackwood's mind raced, connecting invisible threads between this new information and the supernatural events he had just witnessed.

"To think," he mused aloud, "that the veil between worlds might be thinner in the drawing rooms of Mayfair than in the graveyards of Whitechapel."

He set the letter down, his fingers drumming a thoughtful rhythm on the desktop. The promise of rest that had lured him home now seemed a distant luxury, overshadowed by the tantalizing prospect of a new mystery.

"Well, my dear Watson," Blackwood said to the empty room, a habit born of countless nights spent in solitary contemplation, "it appears our work is far from done."

Blackwood leaned back in his chair, the worn leather creaking beneath him. The flickering lamplight cast dancing shadows across his face, accentuating the lines etched by years of confronting the inexplicable. He closed his eyes, allowing the weight of recent events to settle upon him like a heavy cloak.

"Loss," he murmured, the word hanging in the air like a ghostly whisper. "How many times have I walked hand in hand with it?"

His mind drifted to Lady Ravenscroft's fading spirit, a poignant reminder of the ephemeral nature of life and the enduring power of truth. A rueful smile played at the corners of his mouth.

"And yet, redemption follows closely behind," Blackwood mused, his voice barely audible. "For her, for me... perhaps for us all."

He opened his eyes, gazing at a small photograph on his desk. It showed Evelyn Bradshaw, her keen eyes gleaming with determination, and Agnes O'Reilly, her kind face radiating warmth even in sepia tones.

"What a trio we made," Blackwood chuckled softly. "The skeptic, the nurturer, and the bridge between worlds."

He reached out, tracing the outline of their faces with a gentle finger. "Evelyn, your relentless pursuit of truth... Agnes, your unwavering compassion... How different this journey would have been without you both."

A sudden gust of wind rattled the windowpane, startling Blackwood from his reverie. He rose, crossing to the window to secure the latch. A familiar silhouette caught his eye as he peered out into the fog-shrouded street.

"Evelyn?" he called out, throwing open the window. "Is that you?"

The figure turned, revealing not Evelyn's face but that of a stranger who quickly melted back into the mist. Blackwood shook his head, chuckling at his own eagerness.

"Perhaps it's time for rest after all," he said to himself, closing the window. "Though I suspect our paths will cross again soon enough, my friends. There are still truths to be uncovered, and I fear London's secrets are far from exhausted."

Blackwood's piercing blue eyes traced the swirling patterns of fog as it danced around the gaslit streets below. The mist seemed to possess a life of its own, coiling and uncoiling like a great serpent, obscuring and revealing glimpses of the cobblestone paths in turn. He leaned closer to the windowpane, his breath leaving a faint patch of condensation on the glass.

"What mysteries do you conceal tonight, old friend?" he murmured to the fog-laden city.

As if in response, a gust of wind sent eddies of mist spinning, momentarily parting to reveal a shadowy figure darting between two buildings.

Blackwood's hand instinctively tightened on the window frame, his keen Detective's instincts prickling.

"Another lost soul, or something more sinister?" he wondered aloud, his voice barely above a whisper.

He turned from the window, pacing the length of his modest lodgings. The lamp's warm glow cast his shadow long against the wall, seeming to stretch into the realm of the unknown.

"The veil between worlds grows thin," Blackwood mused, his thoughts churning. "With each case solved, another mystery emerges from the shadows. It's a delicate balance, this dance between the seen and unseen."

He paused, running a hand through his tousled dark hair. "And yet, is it not our duty to pierce that veil? To shine a light into the darkest corners of both man and spirit?"

Blackwood's gaze fell upon his well-worn Detective notebook lying open on his desk. He picked it up and thumbed through pages filled with observations of the mundane and the supernatural.

"The pursuit of truth is a never-ending journey," he said softly, a hint of determination creeping into his voice. "Each answer begets new questions; each revelation unveils new mysteries."

He closed the notebook with a decisive snap.

"And so, the game continues. London's secrets may run deep, but my resolve runs deeper still. Whatever hidden dangers lurk in the shadows, whatever untold stories await discovery, I shall face them."

Blackwood returned to the window, his reflection ghostly in the glass. The fog continued its ceaseless dance, a constant reminder of the unknowable forces at work in the world.

"The night is long," he whispered, a faint smile playing at the corners of his mouth, "but dawn always comes. And with it, new adventures, new challenges to overcome."

As he spoke, a distant church bell tolled midnight, its somber notes drifting through the misty air. Blackwood straightened, squaring his shoulders as if preparing for battle.

"Come what may," he declared to the silent room and the sleeping city beyond, "I shall stand ready. For in the pursuit of justice and truth, there can be no rest, no respite. The unknown beckons, and I... I must answer its call."

Don't miss out!

Visit the website below and you can sign up to receive emails whenever David L. Waters publishes a new book. There's no charge and no obligation.

https://books2read.com/r/B-A-JCBLC-RMAJF

BOOKS 2 READ

Connecting independent readers to independent writers.

Also by David L. Waters

Mystery in the Harbor
Echoes of the Past: Detective Arthur Blackwood's Haunting Case in Victorian London
Veil of Shadows: The Case of the Order of the Eternal Flame
Whispers from the Docks
The Treasure of Port Vigil
Echoes of Ravenscroft

About the Author

David Waters, a 67-year-old retired Navy veteran, has lived a life marked by dedication, bravery, and service to his country. Born in 1957 in Charleston, South Carolina, David grew up with an intense patriotism and a desire to serve. This calling led him to enlist in the United States Navy at 21.

After six years of honorable service, David was discharged from the Navy in 1984. His retirement did not mark the end of his contributions, however. David became an active member of veteran organizations, advocating for the rights and welfare of fellow veterans. He also dedicated time to mentoring young sailors and sharing his knowledge and experience.

Now, at 67, David is embarking on a new adventure: a writing career he has long dreamed of. With a passion for storytelling and a wealth of experiences to draw from, David is excited to share his stories with the world. His writing focuses on naval history, personal memoirs, and fictional tales inspired by his adventures at sea.